how to fall in love with a demon

DECEIT & DEVOTION

LOLA GLASS

Cover by Fenix Cover Design
https://fenixcoverdesigns.com

To my husband:

This is what happens when you tell me to embrace being a hurricane

Prison

Scale Ridge

Wildwood

Wolfcrest

Cub Lake

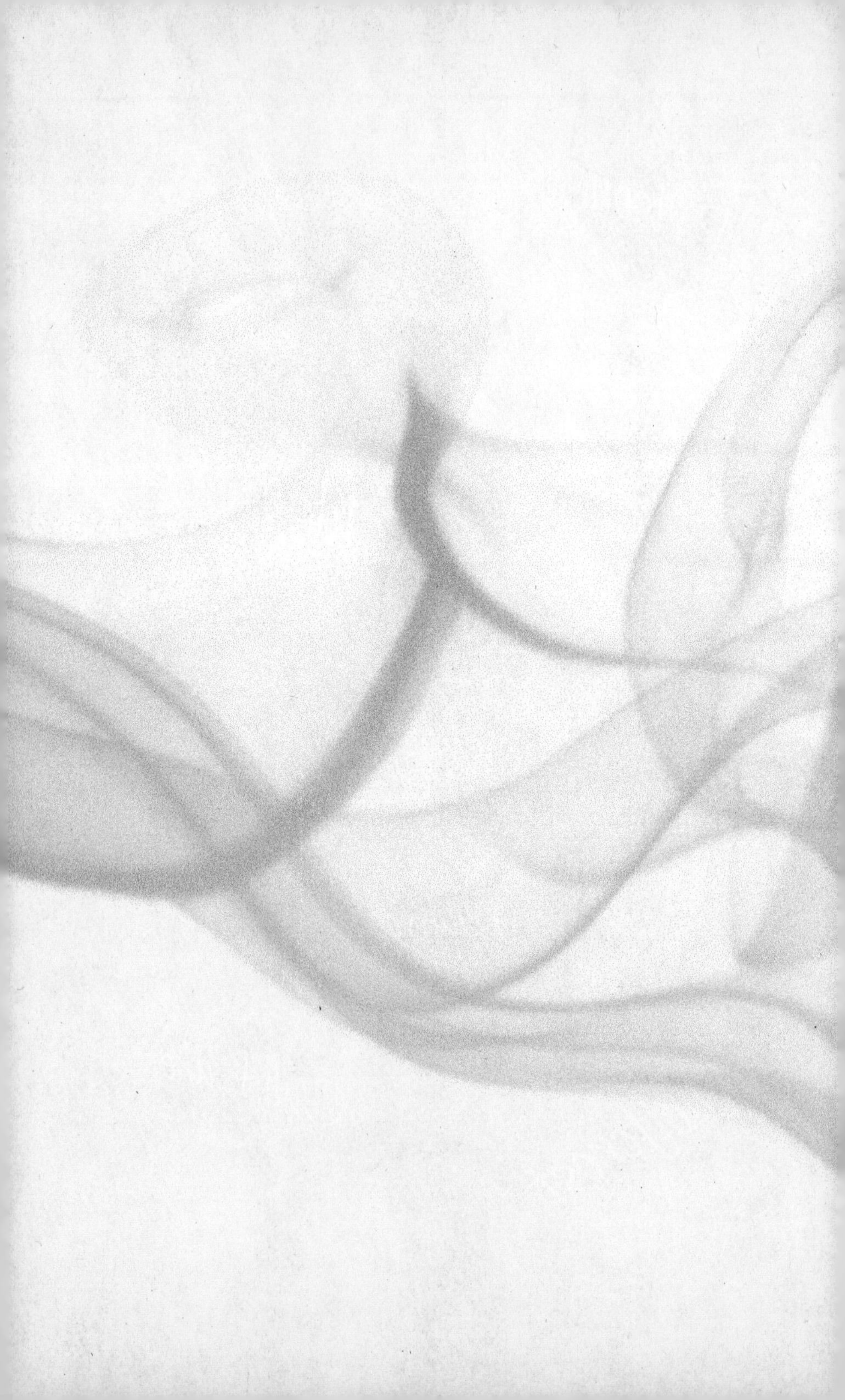

one

TATUM

THE SMELL of coffee was thick in the air as I took a big bite of my newest attempt at the perfect peppermint truffle. Rich flavor flooded my mouth, but I made a face.

Still not perfect yet.

I'd tweak the amount of—

"Oh, it can't be that bad." My favorite barista, Sophie, plucked one off the plate and took a bite.

"Damn, Tatum." Her groan made my lips curve upward. "I'll marry you, if you'll take me."

She was perky, pale, blonde, and in a serious relationship with her high school sweetheart, so we both knew she was joking. Sophie was twenty-one, and I wasn't all that much older than her at twenty-four, so we got along well.

"I'll consider it."

She slowly ate the rest of the chocolate while Hector, the other barista working, finished the drink for the customer waiting near the counter.

I tucked a few loose strands of long, cinnamon-colored hair behind my ear and added a couple notes to the side of my recipe card. They were ideas for a few possible tweaks in case the ones I had planned didn't work out, and each of them would need their own test batch.

My phone buzzed while I was writing, and I pulled it from my pocket to read the text.

MILES

How did the truffles come out?

ME

Eh

BRYNN

In Tatum-speak, that means they're almost perfect

ME

Almost, being the key word

BRYNN

You'll figure it out. Keep us updated!

I sent a thumbs-up, and tucked my phone back into the pocket of my half-apron. Sophie had stepped into the front of the shop and was helping a new customer, while Hector stole a truffle of his own.

"Tatum's working in the kitchen. What do you need her for?" Sophie's voice lifted, the tone telling me I needed to get my ass to her side, so I strode to the front of my coffee shop without hesitating.

The most gorgeous man I'd ever seen stood across from her. He had to be six and a half feet tall, and was built entirely out of muscle. His skin was tan and his wavy, black hair fell nearly to his chin, a little too long and messy to be considered purposeful. He wore what looked like black scrubs that had seen much, much better days.

His eyes?

They were glowing red.

My mind went back to the high school classes I'd been forced to take about supernatural beings. They had come out of hiding two centuries earlier, and after a short war, a peace treaty was created.

They had lived among us peacefully (for the most part) ever since, but it was still important to know enough about them not to do anything stupid when we came across them. While it wasn't hard to avoid the places they frequented, even werewolves needed to buy groceries.

And this guy had glowing red eyes, which meant...

Demon.

He was a demon.

A *hungry* demon, if I remembered correctly. Demons and vampires were like two sides of the same coin—vampires fed on blood, and demons fed on lust.

So why was he in my coffee shop?

The man looked over his shoulder, like he expected to find someone behind him.

That was odd.

"How can I help you?" I asked the demon, my voice polite but not friendly. Being too friendly in a coffee shop only led to guys leaving behind business cards and phone numbers I didn't ask for.

The man leaned over the counter a little, toward me, not Sophie.

She took a few steps back, and I didn't blame her. She was tiny.

While I wasn't exactly intimidating, coming in at 5'6", I was built strong, not skinny. My best friends and I had taken a few self-defense classes just to be safe, too. Not that they would be useful against a demon man who was legitimately a foot taller than me.

The man's hands landed on the counter, and my gaze dipped to them. The bastard had an artist's fingers—long and elegant, though just as strong as the rest of him.

"There's a dragon shifter outside this coffee shop," the man said, his voice low and smooth.

Goosebumps erupted on my arms, and I was glad I'd worn an oversized sweater that hid them from him. It was fall in our city, Scale Ridge, nestled in the foothills of a massive mountain range, which meant the cold was getting real.

Dragon shifters were supposed to be fairly safe. They defended a prison deep in the mountains that held those who broke the supernatural government's laws. Truthfully, a dragon shifter sounded much safer than a red-eyed demon to me.

"Okay..." I studied the man.

I couldn't glare at him or kick him out without reason; supernaturals were known for being powerful in many ways. The guy didn't look famous, like some of them were, but that didn't mean he wasn't powerful.

Treating a supernatural poorly, with or without reason, could lead to my shop getting shut down.

Hell, it could lead to getting *murdered.*

Usually, I stayed out of the bars, nightclubs, and gyms that were known to be run by supernaturals. So usually, I didn't have to worry about them.

"He expects me to walk out with my mate," the demon said.

His *mate*?

Mating was the supernatural version of marriage. I would definitely have known if anyone I worked with was mated to a demon. I wouldn't have asked outright, but people talked about that shit.

"I don't think he or she is here. I can get you coffee, or homemade candy. That's all we have for sale." I tapped the logo on the display case. It said *Coffee & Toffee*, the name of my shop.

The man caught my hand, and I went still. A pulse of *something* rolled through my veins, relaxing my body somehow. My fear was gone, and I was no longer worried about the fact that there was a glowing-eyed demon in my shop.

"Let go of her, or I'll call the police," Sophie warned from behind me.

The demon released my arm. "Be my mate," he said.

Was he kidding?

He had to be kidding.

His magic had relaxed me so much, I couldn't suppress my sarcasm.

"Yes, I'm going to agree to be your mate two minutes after we've met," I drawled.

His lips curved upward, and he said one word. "*Aeternum.*"

I had never heard the word before, but there was something about it.

Something... magical.

My knees knocked together as a wave of something intangible crashed over me.

In one smooth motion, the demon vaulted over the counter.

Sophie gasped.

The demon grabbed me by the waist, his grip iron as he held me upright.

There was pressure in my head, and it made me feel fuzzy.

Very, very fuzzy.

"What did you do to me?" I breathed.

"You agreed to be my mate, Tatum. Two minutes after we met, in fact." His voice was lower than it had been before, edged almost with humor.

I would've assumed he'd read my nametag to learn my name, but he had asked for me specifically. That meant he had come into the shop knowing, at the very least, who I was.

"It was a joke." I tried to push him away, but the moment he released my waist, I nearly crashed to the ground. So, he caught me once again.

"A mate bond doesn't discriminate against sarcasm."

I made a noise of outrage, and tried to push him away again.

He didn't budge at all, despite my efforts.

"When the dragon shifter walks in here, act like you know me. If you don't, he'll drag both of us back to prison with him."

"Prison?" my voice lifted.

Sophie squeaked behind me.

The shop's door opened, and the bell jingled loudly.

My mind was still fuzzy, and my vision was, too.

My head jerked toward the entrance to my coffee shop, anyway.

A shirtless, inked-up man just as big as the demon holding me upright stalked into the room. His skin was golden-brown, and his hair was dark blond. His narrowed eyes went automatically to me, and I found myself leaning into the demon just a little more.

"Villin," the dragon shifter growled.

"My mate, as promised." The demon stepped behind me, his strong chest and abdomen pressed to my back. I sucked in a breath at the contact—and the possessive hand he spread over my ribs, just below my breasts.

Wait, was his name Villin?

As in, *villain*?

That didn't sound good.

"Tatum, this is August. He's the pain in the ass who has kept me from you this past year."

And, *past year*?

Had he seriously been in the supernatural prison for a year?

The dragon studied me. "How long have you been together?"

I opened my mouth to tell the dragon it was a lie, but the demon's—*Villin's*—nose brushed the side of my throat, and my head tilted just a little in that direction. It caught me off guard enough that the words died in my throat as he all but purred into my ear, "*Lie*, Tater-tot."

The nickname was enough to make me scowl, but I did lie. The threat of prison while a demon's arms were around me was plenty to encourage that. "Long enough."

The dragon didn't look angry at or surprised by my answer. "Show me your hands."

Villin lifted my right hand with his, and I tried not to gasp audibly when I saw the shimmering, swirling black markings that curled around my fourth finger and spread over the back of my hand. The way the demon was holding it told me the marks were on my palm, too.

The dragon's face twisted in a snarl. "You know the rules, Villin."

With that, he turned and stormed out of the shop.

I couldn't suppress my shudder as he left, and immediately squirmed away from Villin. He released me, though he seemed like he was watching to make sure I didn't collapse again.

The fog in my mind had vanished, and my thoughts were returning to normal. There was an ache in my stomach that hadn't been there before—hunger, I thought—but it had been a while since I ate, so I paid no mind to it.

"What is going on?" I demanded, tossing a hand toward the door of my coffee shop. "Your name is *Villin*? We're mated? And what the hell is *this*?" I held up my hand, which was trembling a little, showing him the gunmetal-colored marking.

"My name is *Rafael* Villin, yes, we are mated, and that is a mate mark." He leaned past me and grabbed one of our branded boxes, then opened the display case. An assload of candy went into the box quickly, without an ounce of organization, before he closed the display case again. "And now, we're leaving."

"I'm not going anywhere," I shot back. "That is *not* enough. You haven't explained anything. Why were you in prison? What are the rules the dragon shifter was talking about? How do we get *un*mated?"

"I will call the cops if I need to," Sophie threw out, though she was about as far from me and *Rafael* Villin as she could get while still remaining in the front of the shop.

"My brothers and I work for the human government, so go ahead." He took a bite of one of the truffles—a pumpkin spice one—then eyed it with surprise. "That's actually pretty good."

I scoffed at the obvious insult behind his compliment.

"I'll explain on the way home. Let's go." He stepped out from behind the counter, striding toward the door and waving me after him.

"We are not together." I gestured between us. "I'm not going anywhere with you."

The glow in his eyes grew brighter, and I heard Sophie suck in a breath.

My phone started buzzing in my apron pocket again—I was getting a phone call—but I ignored it.

"What's it going to take to get you in the car, Tater-tot?" Rafael asked.

"An explanation? Answers? I don't know." My phone started buzzing again, so I lifted it to my ear and answered it without looking to see who it was. "Hello?"

"I just heard that a *dragon shifter* landed near your shop. Are you okay?" Miley checked.

"Okay is relative. I'll call you back."

"No, Tatum, wait—"

I hung up, but held my phone in my hand as if it could help me somehow.

It couldn't.

The demon's eyes narrowed. "Who was that?"

"My friend."

"A *boy*friend?"

"That's none of your business." Annoyance had me silencing my phone before tucking it in the pocket of my jeans. "Answer my questions, and I'll consider going with you." After a short pause, I added quickly, "Assuming I agree that I need to. Also, you have to pay for those."

"Mates can't be apart for the first few years after the bond is formed. Distance leads to psychosis."

Well, that was just fantastic.

"How do we *un*mate, then?"

"We don't. A sealed mate bond is unbreakable."

Silence reigned in the shop.

I glanced backward, and did a double-take when I saw Sophie standing still with a peaceful look on her face. "What did you do to her?" My voice was sharp, and worried. "Undo it."

"I just got out of *prison*, Tater-tot. I've been starving for months. I can't control my drain on anyone's emotions when I'm this hungry, which is why I'm trying to get you out of this damn coffee shop."

Shit.

I was going to have to go with him.

Letting out a long breath, I finally untied my apron.

"Do *not* call me that again. I'll go with you to my apartment, so we can talk away from everyone else."

"I need my clothes, woman. And money, if you want me to pay you." He lifted the box of candy.

"I'm not going to your house." I hung my apron up and grabbed my purse. After tucking my newest recipe card in the bag, I threw it over my shoulder and strode toward the door. "And I'm driving."

"Good. I rode here on a dragon."

I bit back a snort.

It was definitely the wrong situation for a joke.

I'd been mated to a demon who hadn't answered any important questions—one who just escaped prison.

And he was hungry for candy, and lust.

Hell, maybe it *was* the time for a joke.

two
TATUM

THE DEMON FOLDED HIS MASSIVE, muscular body into my reliable SUV with surprising ease.

But wow, the vehicle felt much smaller with him in the passenger seat. If I moved to the side more than an inch or two, my shoulder would hit his.

Yikes.

I started my car and began driving.

On second thought, taking him back to my apartment was probably a terrible idea. I didn't want him to know where I lived, or what my place looked like.

Then again, it was a worse idea to let him take me to his home—wherever it was—because he would have more control there.

Anywhere public was out because of his magic, so my apartment was the best of the bad options.

"Can I borrow your phone?" he asked me, eating his way through the stolen candies like he was starving. His eyes were glowing, so maybe he was.

"Not until you've answered my questions." I adjusted my hands on the steering wheel, worried he'd flip out at me or try to drain my emotions like he had Sophie's and Hector's.

"Alright, go ahead." He sounded like he was just humoring me.

"There's no way to unmate us?"

"No, despite many centuries of effort from many of the most obnoxious witches on the planet."

My nose wrinkled at the mention of witches.

Everyone hated witches.

Honestly, I wasn't even sure why. They were just hated.

"Then why did you mate with me?"

"Because my options were eternity with you, or in a cell."

Right.

The prison thing.

"What did you do to end up in prison? And why did you have to choose between mating or jail?"

"I told you, I work for your government. My brothers and I hunt vampires who're killing humans. As long as we clean up after ourselves, the supernatural government turns a blind eye. We took down a high-profile vamp after she'd slaughtered a group of humans, and even though we had evidence that she'd broken the laws, the government got involved. I took the fall for it so my brothers would stay free, and ended up in prison."

I blinked. "So you *murder* vampires?"

Was I being purposefully obtuse?

Yes.

It was much easier to label him as an actual villain at the moment than to accept he was protecting people.

"Only the bad ones."

I scowled. "Murder is murder, Rafael. The prison exists to hold those vampires."

"Agree to disagree." He took another bite of a chocolate. "Who made these?"

"My chef," I grumbled.

He didn't need to know that *I* was my chef.

"You'll need to get me their number. I've never had anything like this before."

The compliment would've meant more to me if he hadn't just used my joke to seal a mate bond between us. And drained my favorite barista's emotions in the process.

At least he wouldn't be out to kill me, since I wasn't a vampire. That was a plus.

"So why did they let you out of prison?"

"My brothers and I have had plans in place for these situations for years. I knew I had a potential mate in Scale Ridge, so I lived here throughout the trial and claimed a shortened sentence for the sake of mating. Mates are respected in the supernatural community, and mated pairs live by different rules. No one takes a mate lightly."

"Except you, apparently," I tossed back.

He lifted a shoulder. "Better than prison."

"For you, maybe."

He was quiet for a moment.

I thought maybe he felt guilty, but when I looked over, I found him wearing an orgasmic-expression while enjoying my take on peanut butter cups.

Bastard.

"You're human," Rafael finally said. "Or you were, anyway. Have you heard of potential mates?"

"No."

"Supernatural beings can't just choose anyone out of a crowd to spend their life with, like humans can. We have a handful of potential mates that we come in contact with through our lives. Most demons move to a new city or country when a pull to a new potential mate begins, because we're not usually interested in taking mates. It's a sign that our magic has found someone else's it's compatible with, and nothing more."

I blinked. "I'm human. I don't have magic."

"Humans are powerful in their own ways. Some are skilled with words, or paint. Others are great speakers, good friends, or loving parents. There are many forms of magic—and all are worth protecting."

His gaze was on the box in his hands as he pulled out another candy.

I tried not to look at him with surprise, because he'd shocked the hell out of me with that last comment.

"And anyway, you're not human anymore. You're bound to me, so you're a demon. You'll need to feed like I do, or you'll start losing control."

Just like that, I was back to hating him. "What? I thought supernaturals were born, not made?"

He chuckled. "That's a lie spread to stop humans from hunting us down to become like us."

Great.

That was just *great.*

"How do you turn someone into a demon, then?"

"Demons can only be made through mating. All it takes to create a vampire, though, is to drain a human with a few drops of vampire blood in their system. They're the easiest to turn."

"And the hardest to control?" Even I had heard about vampire attacks in the past. They were rare, but they did happen.

"Exactly."

We parked in front of my apartment, and Rafael lifted a critical eye to the building. The fourplex was small and simple, but the landscaping was kept up with for the most part. "Not much for security, are you?"

I wanted to punch him in the face.

I really, really did.

While it was nothing fancy, it was cheap enough that when we moved in, my roommates and I could pay off our business and education debts quickly. The last of us had paid off the final chunk of debt a few months earlier, and we had celebrated by going on a trip to Hawaii. It had been a blast, and it felt good to be free that way.

We still didn't want to pay for a nicer apartment, though. I was saving up for a house, Miles was investing, and Brynn wasn't sure what she was stockpiling money for.

"Not all of us get paid the big bucks to murder supernaturals," I shot back, unbuckling my seatbelt and stepping out of the car. Rafael followed me up to my door, which was on the bottom floor of the complex. He carried his now-empty box of candy with him.

I unlocked the door and stepped inside. My roommates and I kept the place clean, and while it wasn't anything fancy, we'd decorated it with the same laid-back, boho vibes we decorated our coffee shops with.

There was another box of candy on the countertop, so of course, Rafael went right for it.

"How can you eat that much chocolate? Don't demons drink lust?" I asked him. Despite everything, I no longer felt like I was in danger with him.

I was just very, very annoyed.

And maybe a little hateful.

"Lust keeps our magic alive and kicking, not our bodies. Food and water handles that. Emotions are enough to keep us breathing, but little more."

"That doesn't tell me why you're gorging yourself on candy."

He lifted his red eyes to me.

They were definitely brighter than they had been the last time I looked at them.

"I'm gorging myself on candy because I haven't eaten what I want in a year, Tater-tot. And now that we're mated, all I want is *you.*"

Oh.

Ohhh.

My face heated. "I am *not* having sex with you."

"I didn't ask you to, did I?" He took another bite of the candy without breaking eye contact.

Right.

He hadn't.

"How do you usually eat?"

"It's not difficult. Nightclubs are usually full of people oozing lust. Bars too, sometimes. Even restaurants, if you get lucky. Strip clubs work, but I'm not a fan. My brothers and I usually go with nightclubs, to make things simple."

"So if I take you to your home, we can go our separate ways, and you can hit up the nearest nightclub?" I checked, hoping he would agree.

Rafael chuckled and lifted his palm, showing me the shimmering marking on his right hand. "If only it worked that way."

I heaved a sigh. "What's the alternative, then?"

"You're going to give me your phone so I can let my brothers know I'm free and mated. We're going to pack your things, and move you into my apartment. I have a spare room, before you panic and assume I'm expecting you to sleep with me."

I flashed him a glare.

He continued anyway. "You're the only person who can feed me now; thank you, mate bond." He waved his hand toward me again. "So, I'm going to have one of my brothers pick up a vibrator on their way here, which you will use with a door between us, so you feel safe, and I don't have to starve."

My face was bright red, and my anger flared hotly. "You assume I don't have a vibrator?"

His eyes moved slowly down my figure, and back up. "I would put money on you not having a vibrator, Tater-tot."

"Asshole." I grabbed a pillow off the couch and threw it at him. Rafael didn't bother to duck or step to the side, letting it hit him on the arm before it fell to the floor.

"It's not assholery; it's logic. I can see lust. We're mated, so it's inevitable that we're attracted to each other. Need is curling off me like I'm a damn sauna right now, yet you're ignoring your own desire so completely that I haven't seen one tiny tendril of it. I know the bond wouldn't connect us if you weren't attracted to me, so the only reasonable conclusion is that you're ignoring it. And doing so impressively well, I might add."

"Or you're wrong about the bond," I shot back.

"Show me your vibrator, then."

The urge to punch him grew stronger.

I lived with two roommates, and our walls were thin. It seemed like an awkward thing to have or do, given the situation. I felt so uncomfortable every time I heard one of my roommates pull theirs out, that I didn't dare try with my own.

He chuckled, the sound low and smooth. Even his voice was seductive. "I'm not judging you for it, Tater-tot. Lust is only one emotion, and it's far from the most important one. The fact that you keep yours in check tells me you have a strong will and a stronger mind, which are among the sexiest qualities you could possess. But it won't kill you to relax a little, either."

"Do *not* send your brothers to the store. I will buy my own vibrator," I said, through gritted teeth.

"I'll order it. Stopping at a store isn't a good idea right now."

"Fine." I sat down on the arm of the couch, hoping it would help me regain my composure and make the urge to punch him disappear. The man was massive, and a vampire murderer on top of that, so there was no way my self-defense skills would be enough to help me win a fight with him. "But I still haven't agreed to feed you yet."

"I'll convince you. Toss me your phone?" He held out his hands, finally free of candy.

I absolutely didn't want to—and knew it had been blowing up with my best friends' phone calls—but since he'd been straight-up about how much lust he was feeling, I figured it was better to just throw the phone at him.

He caught it easily, unlocked it after I reluctantly gave him the code, and typed the number quickly before lifting it to his ear. His gaze lingered on me as he grabbed another chunk of toffee, so I turned my head just to avoid more eye contact.

The phone started ringing, and my head jerked toward him.

He'd put it on speaker?

"Don't want you thinking I'm planning your murder," he said, flashing me a small grin.

I glared back, though I had to put in effort not to grin.

"Hello?" A smooth, low voice answered the phone.

"It's me," Rafael said.

"Rafe's out," the other voice called loudly.

Rafe?

It fit him better than Rafael, at least.

"Did he find his female?" another guy asked.

I scoffed.

The disdain in his voice was enough to make me want to punch him, too.

"Yes, I found her. She's holding me captive in her apartment right now, but eventually I'll talk her into going back to my place."

"Have you convinced her to feed you yet?"

"Not really. She's got fire."

I'd take that one as a compliment.

"We'll grab you some groceries and come by to stock your place," one of the guys said.

"Thanks." He hung up the phone, glancing down at the screen. His eyes narrowed, the glow in them brightening. "Who the fuck is Miles, and why has he called you a dozen times in the past half hour?"

Rafael assumed Miles was a man. And that I was sleeping with him.

And he was jealous? Seriously? We'd just met.

"Like I said, it's none of your business who I spend time with."

"We're mated, Tater-tot. If you have a boyfriend, you end it now."

"Why would I end a relationship for a demon who walked into my coffee shop and basically forced me to mate with him?" I shot back.

"I didn't *force* anything." His smooth voice took on a bit of a growl. I liked the grit in it more than I would admit.

"I was being sarcastic when I agreed, and you know it."

"I'm not going to apologize for making you mine. Not to you, or your ex," he all but growled back.

"Are you seriously jealous?" My eyebrows lifted, my voice incredulous. "You don't even know me."

"I don't need to know you. You agreed to the bond in a roundabout way, and that makes you mine, whether you like it or not. I—"

Both of our heads snapped toward the door when we heard a key in the lock. It flew open, and one of my best friends stepped inside, her eyes wild and worried. She had pale skin, was barely 5'1", and her curly black hair was the biggest part of her. Her body was lean with muscle, thanks to her obsession with yoga, which her black leggings and tight, cropped gray top showed off.

"What happened, Tatum?" she demanded, her gaze landing on me before moving to Rafael, where they halted abruptly. "Who the hell are you?"

"Miles, meet Rafael. Rafael, this is my friend, *Miley*." I emphasized her full name.

His expression relaxed, moving between us.

"What are you doing in our apartment, Rafael?" Miles crossed the room, leaving the door open as she stepped up to my side.

"My mate brought me here. I tried to convince her otherwise," he said, much more calm than he'd been a moment earlier.

"Your *what*?" Her gaze jerked to me.

"Apparently, you should never give a sarcastic answer when a demon asks you to be his mate."

She blinked once, and then again. "Shit."

"Yeah." I ran my fingers through my hair.

I was getting hungrier, and wasn't sure what to do about it. If Rafe was right, I might have been hungry for more than just *food*.

"What do we do?" She looked back at Rafael, and her shoulders slowly relaxed.

Her expression did too.

"Don't drain her emotions," I snapped at the demon.

"I told you, I have no control around humans right now." His voice was calm, but his words were clipped.

"Think I need to sit down," Miles murmured.

I grabbed her arms when she stumbled, and helped ease her onto the couch.

“Brynn’s on her way too.” She leaned back against the cushions. “That demon really packs a punch.”

“I’m taking him back to his place,” I agreed quickly, standing as soon as I was sure she wasn’t going to fall off the couch. When I gestured toward Rafe, he grabbed the candy box off the countertop and strode out of the apartment with it.

“Be careful. I’ll keep an eye on your shop. Call us if you need help,” Miley mumbled.

“Will do,” I lied.

I wouldn’t let them near Rafael until he was in control of his magic again... and he wouldn’t be in control again until I agreed to feed him.

So, it would probably be a while.

A long, long while.

But hey, at least he only believed in murder when it came to vampires.

three

TATUM

RAFE and I were both silent as he navigated us to his apartment. The only noise in the car was him telling me when and where to turn. He didn't touch the candy again during the drive, which seemed like a miracle after the way he'd been inhaling it earlier.

My fingers tightened on the steering wheel with our first turn into the expensive part of the city.

They tightened again when he guided me into the parking garage of one of the sleekest, newest buildings in the area.

And again when he had me park my sensible white SUV between multiple vibrantly-colored luxury cars.

I left the vehicle running for a minute, staring at the wall of the parking garage in front of me.

"Are you going to turn the car off?" Rafael asked me, nudging my arm lightly.

"Haven't decided," I said.

He waited another minute.

I didn't move.

"Tater-tot?"

"So you're rich?" I finally asked.

"Yup."

I let out a long breath.

I'd known that. Supernatural beings were immortal, for the most part—they had more time to make money, and magical skills that were more valuable than the rest of ours.

Still, it made me even less certain than I already was.

Rafe leaned over and turned my car off, grabbing the keys and stepping out of the car.

"Damn demon," I muttered under my breath, carefully opening my own door and sliding out. I maintained a solid six-inch gap between my door and the Lamborghini next to it, not willing to risk getting any closer.

"If you can afford to live here, you can afford to pay for the candy you stole," I told him, hurrying to catch up.

"Finally recovered from the shock?"

"Shut up."

His lips curved upward.

We stepped into a fancy elevator, and he typed a code into a keypad. A green light lit up, and it rose smoothly.

"Not going to ask how rich, are you?" he asked me.

"Not interested."

I *was* interested.

I wasn't going to admit it, though.

Rafe eyed me. "We forgot to pack your stuff."

"I didn't forget anything. I haven't agreed to move in with you."

"Ah."

"Mmhm."

"I'll send my brothers for it," he said.

"Not if you want a chance at convincing me to feed you."

He grimaced, but didn't argue.

The elevator dinged, and the doors opened to a small hallway with two doors that faced each other. Rafe typed a code into the keypad on the door to the left, and it opened into a huge living space.

My eyes rounded as I took everything in. The colors and décor weren't modern, but they were simple and comfortable. The floors were a rich shade of brown, the walls a soft white, and the kitchen cabinets a natural wood shade that made me feel at home. Any chef would be happy working in a kitchen that big, with appliances that gorgeous.

The walls in front of me were massive, floor-to-ceiling windows that gave a stunning, unencumbered view of the mountains. There were only two gaps in the windows. One was for a huge bookshelf, and the other was for a movie-theater-worthy TV.

My eyes followed the huge windows up to a second floor that looked like it only covered about half the living space of the one we were on. Was it a loft? I wasn't sure. It gave half the living room monstrously-high ceilings, though, which was gorgeous.

Along the staircase leading up to it and the ledge that looked out at the living area, there were metal rails. They were done in a matte black shade that matched the handles on the kitchen cabinets, and tied the whole space together.

"The bedrooms are upstairs." Rafe gestured to a staircase, and then in another direction as he set the candy box on the countertop. "The bathroom down here is over there, and the remote should be on the side table if you want to turn the TV on. Yell for me if I don't hear my brothers come in." With that, he headed toward the stairs.

"You never gave me my phone back," I reminded him.

He stopped, pulled my phone from his pocket, and tossed it to me before heading up the stairs.

"Let me know if you decide to strip down and touch yourself. I'm still hungry," he called over his shoulder.

My face flushed, but I resisted grabbing a pillow to throw at him that time.

Ignoring him, I stepped out of my shoes and strode over to the couch. It was a monstrous thing, in a shade of blue that almost reminded me of denim.

When I plopped down on it, I decided my new life goal was to make enough money to buy a couch that comfortable for my own house.

After I bought said house, of course.

I didn't bother with the TV, instead calling Miley back. I heard a shower turn on, and felt more relaxed knowing that Rafael was occupied. The phone rang twice before she answered.

"You're still alive?" Miles asked.

"Seems like it," I said relaxing into the couch. "How are you feeling?"

"Really good, actually," she admitted. "I didn't realize how nice it would be to have no emotions for a minute. I haven't felt this relaxed in years."

"I'm glad." I closed my eyes and let out a long breath.

"So what happened, exactly?" Brynn asked. It didn't surprise me to hear her; we always put each other on speaker when two of us were together and the other was on the phone.

I gave them both a quick rundown of meeting Rafe, followed by the dragon shifter, and everything else that had gone down.

"You're not in danger, then?" Miley checked.

"I don't think so. There's a chance he could want to kill me just so he doesn't have to deal with having a mate, but he'd probably end up back in prison if he did. Apparently, mate bonds are sacred to supernaturals."

"That's not entirely reassuring," Miley said.

"Believe me, I know." I squeezed my eyes shut tighter.

"What does his place look like?" Brynn asked, curiosity in her voice.

"Gorgeous," I admitted, opening my eyes and taking in the breathtaking view of the mountains. It was late in the afternoon, but the sun hadn't started going down yet, so everything was bathed in light.

They convinced me to show them, so we changed it into a video call, and they oohed and ahhed as I showed them everything. It was fun seeing their heads squished together in the camera. Brynn was tall and curvy, with straight blonde hair and tanned skin, so she had to lean down while Miles had to strain upward.

"It's surprisingly comfortable." I turned my video off and leaned my head back against the couch. "But I don't know what I'm going to do about the *feeding him* thing."

"Just read a sexy book or something," Miley suggested. "You don't actually have to orgasm, right? He just needs the lust?"

"I'm not sure."

"Don't you have a vibrator?" Brynn asked.

I grimaced.

Damn the whole vibrator question.

"You don't?" Her voice was incredulous.

"Not everyone needs a vibrator," Miley protested.

"Holy shit, you don't either?" she demanded. "I'm living with sexually-starved women! It's no wonder you always put my dishes in the sink while I'm eating the meal I cooked."

"There's no point in letting the food get all dry and crusty on the dishes," Miles protested.

"They don't get crusty in ten minutes. I—"

I heard someone typing the code in on Rafael's door, and I cut their argument off. "The brothers just got here. Gotta go."

Since I couldn't see over the couch's massive back, I stood up quickly, just so I could see who was walking into the space I had been forced to occupy.

Rafe's shower was still running, and I wasn't about to interrupt it, despite what he'd told me to do.

Two men who looked a hell of a lot like my *mate* stepped into the apartment, both of them looking straight at me.

I stared back.

After a moment, they walked into the kitchen and set all of the grocery bags they were carrying on the counter.

Though their faces were shaped similarly to Rafe's, with the same tan skin and dark hair, they looked a hell of a lot more put-together. And healthier; they looked healthier, somehow.

I couldn't pinpoint exactly what the visual difference was, but looking at them, I could tell it was there. Maybe his skin was slightly... more gray?

That didn't seem right, so I wasn't going to bring it up.

One of them had artfully-messy hair that was cut surfer-style. He wore a light gray sports coat with acid-washed jeans, and a white t-shirt.

The other had his hair cut short on the sides and longer on top, with every strand gelled carefully in place. He was in a black suit and tie, looking sleek and expensive. The man's appearance basically screamed *BUSINESS.*

"You're the barista?" the one with the surfer hair asked.

There wasn't as much disdain in his voice as I'd heard on the phone.

I scowled. "My name is Tatum."

The shower shut off.

"I'm Sebastian. This is Zander. We respect your profession more than he makes it sound," the business one said, gesturing to his brother. "Rafe is in the shower?"

I nodded curtly.

"Did he bring up feeding him?" Zander added.

"He said I had to. I said no." I glanced down at the time on my phone and realized I hadn't checked in to make sure Sophie was okay. "I need to make a few calls."

Sebastian dipped his head, like he understood. Wordlessly, he and Zander headed for the stairs.

I walked to the far end of the apartment, putting as much space between me and the guys as I could before I called the shop's phone number.

Sophie answered quickly, her voice calm. "Coffee & Toffee, this is Sophie."

"Hey, Soph. How are you doing?"

"Oh my gosh, I'm so glad you're okay! I'm fine; the demon's magic actually felt kind of nice. How are you? What happened?"

"I'm still trying to figure that out," I admitted. "Are you still good to work tomorrow?"

"Of course! I already heard from Miley, too, and she's planning to stop by and make sure everything's going well partway through the day."

"Perfect. Thanks for being so awesome." I closed my eyes, leaning the side of my head against the glass. My stomach was starting to ache with hunger, but I really just wanted to collapse in bed and sleep away everything that had happened that day.

Unfortunately, sleeping wouldn't make Rafael or the mate marking on my hand miraculously disappear.

"No problem. Good luck with your demon issues!"

I laughed softly. "Thanks. I'm going to need it." Hanging up the phone, I slipped it in my jeans' pocket again.

I needed time to come up with a plan. Time to think up a way out of everything. Hell, time just to *process* everything and figure out exactly what I was going to do about it.

Time seemed like something I didn't have, though.

Rafe was starving. He needed me to feed him before he could go anywhere with humans—and humans were everywhere. I was hungry too, and probably needed to figure out how to eat like a demon did.

On top of that, I still needed to finish perfecting all three of my seasonal candies for Christmas. It was the beginning of October, so I didn't have much time left.

It was all just... overwhelming.

I turned my head as all three brothers came down the stairs together. Rafael was grinning, dressed in a gray tee that fit him like a second skin and a pair of black joggers. The scruff on his chin had been trimmed to stubble, though his waves were still damp and long. Both of his brothers wore similar expressions.

They all acknowledged me briefly before they gathered in the kitchen and then started putting away groceries together. Remaining where I was, I watched them work.

They moved smoothly, all of them clearly knowing where everything went. To me, that meant they probably spent plenty of time together, and in each other's homes. Or at the very least, at Rafael's place.

"Mom called when we were on the way here. She heard about your bond," the messier one, Zander, said.

"Dammit," Rafe grumbled. "Is she on a plane yet?"

"I talked her into giving it a week. That should give you enough time to get your act together," Sebastian said. "I'm sure she suspects it's fake, but she's smart enough not to ask questions she doesn't want the answer to."

"We'll sell it," Rafe said.

Now he expected me to lie to his mom?

Geez, I had managed to get myself wrapped up in a *great* situation.

At least he was still close with his mother, I supposed. According to a few gossip articles I'd read, some supernatural families were at war with each other and had been for centuries.

"I'll take care of dinner. Zander was halfway through setting up your phone and computer; help him with that." Sebastian glanced sideways at me. "Or go and make sure your mate knows you can't hurt her."

My lips curved downward at his mention of me.

Rafael reached for one of the bags, but Zander grabbed it before he could, hauling it over to the kitchen table. There, he pulled out boxes for a brand new laptop and phone.

Rather than making his way toward me, Rafe grabbed another piece of chocolate from the box.

His brothers noticed the candy, for the first time since they arrived, and both of them beelined straight to it.

Rafael tried to smack their hands away, but they both pulled out a few pieces of chocolate and toffee anyway. I tried not to feel pride with how quickly they staked their claim on the candy, but failed.

"Damn, this is good," Zander said, lifting a surprised gaze my way. "This came from your coffee shop?"

"It did."

"She won't give me the name of the candy chef. I already asked," Rafael said, popping one of the chocolates into his mouth.

Sebastian glanced my way again. "How much do we owe you?"

I honestly had no idea what had been in either of the boxes, so there was no way to guess.

The demons were stupidly rich though, so they could pay whatever I told them.

"Three hundred."

Zander and Sebastian grinned.

Rafe snorted. "You charge interest by the minute, don't you?"

"Yup. And I'll start doubling the interest for every extra insult you throw my way."

"I haven't *insulted* you," he countered.

"Not one for security, are you?" I mimicked him, earning a sheepish grimace.

One of his brothers snorted, but I didn't look away from him long enough to see which. Probably Zander, since I hadn't seen Sebastian show any real sign of emotion yet.

"I was hangry."

"I'm dripping in lust, and you're a dry, cardboard box of a human who's never even seen a vibrator," I said, lowering my voice in an attempt to resemble his smooth timbre. "Do you even know how sex works?"

Sebastian coughed on a laugh, and Zander snorted.

"That is not a quote," Rafael said, lifting a finger.

"It was implied by what you *did* say."

"You can do much better than a hundred bucks per insult from your mate," Zander said with a grin.

"They're not her chocolates," Rafael pointed out. "Technically—"

Sebastian set a hand on his shoulder, hard, cutting him off. "I don't think you want to finish that sentence."

"You really need to eat," Zander said, shooting me an apologetic grin. "Usually, Rafe's the nice one."

"Sure he is." I hoped my deadpanned stare told him exactly how little I believed him.

"Demons typically feed on lust one to two times a week to function at their full capacity." Sebastian released Rafael and went back to the fridge, where he pulled ingredients out. "We're starved in prison so our magic will pull emotions from the other beings around us. It keeps everyone else calm, but only ensures our hearts keep beating. It's survival, but just barely."

That sounded like hell.

But, it didn't mean I was going to offer myself up on a silver platter. Or a pink one, if it involved a vibrator.

"I'm sure it would. Anyway, I'm going to go take a shower," I said, heading toward the stairs before the conversation could get any less comfortable.

"I'll show you to it," Rafael said, catching me as I reached them.

"I know what a bathroom looks like."

"Of course you do. I figured I could get you a pair of my clothes, so you'll be more comfortable," Rafael said, and I could feel his gaze on me as we made our way up the stairs. "It's not cold enough in here for your sweater, boots, or jeans."

"I'm fine, thanks." I didn't look his way.

"I was planning on staying the night here—does that work for you?"

"Since when do you care what works for me?"

There was a moment of tense silence.

We finally reached the bathroom, and I stepped inside, smoothly closing the door behind me. He caught it just before it shut, opening it just enough that our eyes met.

"I know I've fucked this up," he said, his voice low. "I spent the last year in a cell with a fire troll, starving, sweating, and in pain. Believe me, I know I've fucked up in every way a person can. I'm sorry that you've been dragged into it, and I will do everything I can to make it up to you, but right now, I'm a mess. I'm sorry you're dealing with it, but that's the truth."

As much as I didn't like it, I appreciated his blunt honesty. After a moment of silence, he released his hold on the door.

I remained where I was for a minute before finally saying, "I'll take a pair of your clothes, and spend the night here. One night, in separate beds. Maybe that will help you settle."

He dipped his head. "Thank you. I hope it will. Give me a second, and I'll be back with the clothes."

Rafael disappeared.

Less than a minute later, he was back with a small, folded pile of clothing. "I'm not sure what will fit."

"I'll make it work. Thanks." I took the pile, then stepped into the bathroom and shut the door. Letting out a long breath, I closed my eyes and leaned against the thick wood.

I didn't really want to take a shower. I just needed space and time away from the demons to process everything that had happened, and I hadn't been able to come up with another way to get that.

So, to the shower I went.

four
RAFAEL

"I HOPE YOU APOLOGIZED, at the very least," Bash said, whisking something in a bowl.

"I did." I plopped down on one of the barstools. "Tell me you didn't eat all the chocolate."

Every fucking inch of my body hurt. I had never felt like I was dying before our government threw me in their prison, but after a year in hell, I was far too well acquainted with the feeling.

Dropping my head into my hands, I let out a long breath.

I had tracked Tatum down one day, before the dragons hauled my ass to prison, just to get a look at her. I'd wanted an idea of what I would be getting myself into.

Though I'd only been there fifteen minutes, it was long enough to learn that she had a laid-back sarcasm that made her coworkers laugh. That she would remember the most complex, obnoxious coffee orders and make them without batting an eyelash. That she would hand the drinks off with a smile that didn't quite reach her gorgeous green eyes.

I'd held on to the image of her in my mind, obsessing over the poor woman while I suffered. Her reddish-brown hair and cream-colored skin lingered in my thoughts and dreams constantly.

Somehow, she was even more gorgeous than I remembered.

...And she hated me more than I ever expected.

"We ate all the chocolate," Zander said. I heard his ass hit the stool beside mine, and the computer and phone followed.

"Fuck you."

"If you had played your cards right a few hours ago, you could be fucking *her*," he countered.

"I don't have the energy to fuck anyone right now."

"Has the pain spread to your chest yet?" Bash asked, always the reasonable one.

"A few weeks ago."

"Damn."

"Someone is going to have to explain to your Tater-tot exactly what happens to a demon as they starve," Zander said.

I lifted my head. Despite the pain that accompanied every breath, I forced myself to continue breathing evenly. "It's not going to be me." After a moment of silence, I tacked on a reluctant, "And don't call her that."

"I nominate Bash," Zander said, typing something into the computer. Probably my login info. It was a damn good thing he kept track of that stuff for me; my mind felt like mush.

"Seconded," I said.

"Do you really want me alone with your mate long enough to have that conversation?" Bash's voice was blunt.

I considered it for all of a breath before the pit of possessiveness reared its ugly head, and my face twisted in a snarl.

"I'll text it to her. The number you called from earlier was hers, right?" he said, roughly trying to smooth it over. Usually, that was my job. I was the one who dealt with the people; they were the ones who handled everything else. That was what made me expendable enough to spend a year in prison while they kept things running.

My exhaustion was thick enough that his clumsy attempt proved successful. "Yes. Fine." I ran a hand through my hair. It needed to be cut, but that was far from a priority.

Somehow, I needed to seduce my mate—who hated me—so I could feed, first.

I set my arms on the countertop, leaning over it and letting my eyes close.

Damn, I was tired.

The sounds and smells of cooking food melded with the tap of fingers on laptop keys. They would've been soothing, if I was in a different mental and physical state.

I wasn't, though.

Most of my attention was fixed on the shower I could hear running. Sensing exact emotions wasn't in a demon's skillset; the only feeling we could sort from among the others was lust, because we could physically see it. But if I went back up the stairs, I would be able to feel the mass of her emotions through the door and wall.

Zander slid my new phone over to me. "This is ready. Should be exactly the way you left it, though one of the buttons was moved since the last model. The laptop will be a while longer while I transfer your old stuff over."

"Thanks." I grabbed it. It took a minute to get reacquainted with the device, but overall, it was mostly the same.

Navigating immediately to the internet, I pulled up everyone's favorite website for online shopping and quickly pulled up the vibrators.

Scrolling through the list, I tried to decide what Tatum would feel the most comfortable using. There would be a level of awkwardness for her just because it was new, but I hoped she would warm up to it.

Or that she would climb in bed with me, though that seemed unlikely.

"She really doesn't have a vibrator?" Zander asked, his voice amused.

"No. I get the impression she doesn't relax often," I said absently, adding a few different styles to the cart. I'd give her a few to choose from, so she felt more in control.

Black seemed like the safest choice, considering her aversion to sex toys, so I didn't bother with any of the neon pink ones.

After I'd ordered those, I found the coffee shop she worked at on a food delivery site, and ordered the maximum amount of everything they had in stock. Sugar dulled male demons' hunger, so I'd need an assload of the damn things. Even if she did agree to feed me, it would take weeks to fully recover after starving for so long.

"Order me some too," Zander said, still working on my computer.

"Find your own candy shop. I already bought that one out," I grumbled, submitting the order with a hefty tip to convince someone to get it to me quickly. Thankfully, my credit cards hadn't expired while I was gone.

"They have more than one location," Bash said. "I noticed one on Raven Street, after the first time we found your female there."

I typed *Coffee & Toffee* into the search bar, and sure enough, found two more locations.

Knowing my brothers would take their fair share of whatever I ordered, I put in an identical order at the other two shops as well. Hopefully they had the same chef, or at least the same recipes.

"I didn't expect a coffee shop to have good candy," Bash remarked.

"Neither did I," Zander agreed.

"And you didn't try the pumpkin spice truffles. I could've died happy," I said, absentmindedly pulling up the website of the nearest flower shop. Tatum didn't strike me as a woman who would be easily swayed by roses, but I needed something to give her with the vibrators.

I'd need to get her a ring before my mother made it into town, too, but I needed to know what she liked before I could do that. I'd never agreed with the human ideal that a woman would love a piece of jewelry just because her male liked it, and had always felt a woman should have some say in what she wore on her finger.

Then again, most men would've probably known what their woman liked before they proposed.

I hadn't proposed at all, so that was already out of the question.

"You'll have to warn her about the party," Bash said.

"I know. I'll have to teach her how to feed, as well."

"And how to identify her hunger," Zander threw in.

Bash added, "On top of warning her that you'll be in her dreams until you've recovered."

"Didn't think about that one." I grimaced, finishing my order and setting my phone back on the counter. "Catch me up on what's gone on at work."

They both distracted me with stories and explanations, until there was a knock at the door.

Bash hauled in a stack of boxes, and closed it again.

A few minutes later, there was another delivery.

And a few minutes after that, there was a third.

All of them were full of candy and chocolate, thankfully.

We opened a few boxes, spreading them out through the kitchen. There wasn't much counter space left—and there was still a stack of full boxes on my table.

They continued talking, and I continued eating, praying the chocolate would miraculously erase the pain throughout my entire body.

It didn't, but I supposed it didn't hurt any more to hope than it did just to live.

TATUM

WHEN I FINALLY STEPPED OUT OF the shower, I felt like I'd wrapped my mind around what had happened.

For the most part, at least.

Regardless of how it had occurred, I was permanently mated to a demon.

I was becoming a demon because of it.

I was going to have to feed my mate, and feed *from* him.

There was no way around any of those facts, so there was no point in trying to escape them or avoid them. We lived in a world that was very much adapt-or-die, and there wasn't a chance I'd let myself die.

So, I would figure out how to adapt.

Rafael would have to adapt for me too, though. He was just as mated as I was. As soon as I fed him to make his life less shitty, we would be having a conversation about how we were going to make it possible for *both* of us to live our own lives the way we wanted to. I would consider us business partners, if nothing else.

I pulled my own bra and underwear back on, and then tried on the borrowed clothes. His pants fit me for the most part, though I had to tighten the drawstring quite a bit.

His shirt went over my head next. It was way too big, so I bundled the extra fabric and tied a knot with it, leaving it at my hip.

Was it cute?

No, it certainly was not.

But it was functional. That was what mattered, considering the alternative was going out there in my bra. I would've been fine with that if I wasn't mated to a demon who had already admitted how lusty he felt, but I was.

So, no walking around in my bra.

As far as I knew, we could feed each other without having sex or seeing each other naked, so that was hopeful. If it was true, I was definitely going to insist on it.

I found a comb in one of the drawers and tugged it through my wet hair. I'd tried to keep it dry at first, but failed, so I used the shampoo and conditioner I found in the shower. It looked a lot more expensive than the grocery store stuff I used, and smelled nice, so I didn't have a problem with it.

The comb slid through my hair with surprising ease. I wrung the excess water out of it with a towel when it was detangled, messing with the long, cinnamon-colored strands so they weren't *too* perfect.

My makeup was long gone, but all I wore was mascara and eyeliner, anyway. I had never managed to figure out how to get foundation to look right, so I gave up on that years earlier. The little I did wear, I only bothered with because I felt like I had to while working in the coffee shop.

If I was really married to a guy, I would marry one who liked the way I looked with or without makeup.

I tried not to let myself care about the fact that I wasn't sure if Rafael liked the way I looked at all.

Or about the fact that us being mated meant I would likely never have a chance to actually fall in love.

Or that I was going to have to figure out a way to introduce him to my family and everyone else in my life. Or that I'd have to do so without telling them the truth about why we were together.

And that I would probably have to act like I was in love with the bastard.

Nope, I wasn't going to think about any of that shit.

Baby steps.

There was a plan, after all. My growling stomach reminded me of that.

I would feed Rafael, and he would teach me how to feed myself in the demon way. Then, we would come to some kind of conclusion about how we were both going to function now that we were mated. I wasn't going to let him rip me away from the life I'd built from scratch.

Opening the bathroom door, I stepped out and took a deep breath in.

Shit, whatever Sebastian had made smelled *incredible*.

Maybe I wasn't turning into a demon as quickly as I'd thought.

If that was the case, I'd still have to feed Rafael, but we could figure out all of the life stuff before I had to learn how to be a demon. That would definitely, *definitely* make things better for me. Time to adjust would be very much appreciated.

Rafe's glowing red gaze was already on the stairs when I made my way down, and he took my appearance in slowly, like he had no desire to look away.

I noticed something coming off of his skin—some kind of faint, burgundy tendrils that moved in a way that reminded me of smoke.

They grew more visible as I watched him.

Or... maybe as he watched me.

He had told me he was radiating lust. Was that what lust looked like?

My gaze moved quickly to his brothers, to see if they were radiating the same thing. Sebastian nodded a hello, and Zander gave a two-finger wave without looking up from his laptop, but neither of them had the smoke coming off their skin.

"What does lust look like?" I asked aloud, finally looking back at Rafael. The color of the tendrils radiating from him had gotten brighter. I wasn't sure what that meant exactly, and wasn't entirely certain I *wanted* to know.

Rafe didn't answer immediately, his eyes still moving over my figure. It was making me a little self-conscious, not that I'd admit it aloud.

"Red smoke," Sebastian answered, when his brother didn't. "The color grows more vibrant and radiates more as the lust gets stronger. It doesn't have to be strong to feed on it; if we can see it, we can take it. But the more intense it is, the less we need to sate our hunger."

Damn, he was full of information. Much better at answering my questions than Rafael had been earlier.

I tried to come up with another question about demons, but drew a blank.

"For reference, Rafe's about as lusty as it gets right now," Zander added.

Rafael elbowed him in the side. He grunted, but otherwise didn't react.

I finally pulled my gaze off my new mate and looked around the kitchen. My eyebrows shot upward when I saw my shop's boxes everywhere.

Everywhere, everywhere. There were two stacks on the table, and a bunch spread out on the counters, open wide.

"Tell me you didn't rob my coffee shop *again*," I said, the words coming out harsher than I expected. There were so many boxes that, on second glance, there was no way all of it could've come from just my shop.

"He paid this time," Zander said.

"I told you I'd pay for last time, too. I'll even leave enough for your interest." Rafael ran a hand through his hair, dragging the long, wavy locks out of his eyes.

"What is up with you and chocolate?" I gestured to the tower of boxes.

"Sugar eases a demon's hunger. A male's, at least. Female demons' hunger is different than ours," Sebastian explained. "Male demons almost always feel some measure of hunger, so we eat sugar to keep it at bay. Females don't feel it constantly, but when they get hungry, the need is sharp and difficult to ignore."

Great.

That was exactly what I needed. *Sharp* hunger.

Sebastian turned back to whatever he was cooking. "Females also lure men when they're hungry. You're starting to lure."

"Considering Rafe's current reaction, I'd say it's hit him *hard*," Zander added. "Pun intended."

Rafe elbowed him again.

"Fantastic." I walked over to the kitchen table and dropped into a chair, far from the guys. At least my lure wasn't so strong that Rafael's brothers were getting lusty.

The way he'd reacted when he thought Miley was my boyfriend made me think his reaction wouldn't be great if my lure affected his brothers.

"This is almost ready. We'll head out before it gets too much stronger," Sebastian said, lifting a saucepan and expertly pouring it into another bowl. "There should be leftovers to last through tomorrow, too."

"Thanks," I said, when Rafael didn't speak up.

His gaze was still lingering on me, hot, bright, and red. Very, very red.

I didn't look down to check for evidence of how *hard* it had hit him.

"No problem. We'll be happy to come back for dinner again tomorrow if you need us; just let us know," Sebastian said smoothly.

"I'll cook for her tomorrow," Rafael said, his voice low.

I wasn't sure what to say to that, so I didn't say anything.

Neither did his brothers.

I played a stupid game on my phone so I wouldn't have to look at any of them, but Rafe's gaze didn't leave me.

There was a knock at the door after a few minutes, and Sebastian pulled it open. He carried a large box into the apartment, heading toward the table I was sitting at.

His footsteps faltered for a moment, and I heard a noise behind him that reminded me of an animal's growl.

When my gaze lifted to Sebastian, I saw the faintest hint of smoke curling off his skin.

He set the box down where he was, then smoothly walked out of the apartment.

I blinked at the door.

My phone vibrated with a text almost as soon as he was gone.

UNKNOWN

Mix the vegetables into the pasta and sauce, and the food will be ready.

It seemed safe to assume the message was from Sebastian.

"Get out," Rafael told Zander, his voice still dangerously low.

"I'll bring your laptop by tomorrow," Zander said, striding toward the door.

Rafael barely acknowledge the words, his eyes still trained on me.

My heartbeat picked up a little as the door closed behind Zander.

I made my way into the kitchen, heading straight for the vegetables and pasta. My stomach growled loudly as I went.

"I might just be hungry for actual food," I told Rafael, forcing my voice to remain steady as I grabbed the bowl of vegetables. "I'm not going to try to deal with the lust-drinking thing until I've tried to eat the normal way. The reaction could just be because—"

A pair of large hands landed on my hips, and the warmth of the grip cut me off.

My eyes closed, and I dropped the bowl back down on the counter. My fingers found the edge of the thick stone, digging into it lightly.

Almost desperately.

"Physical hunger can't trigger a lure, Tatum." His voice was serious, and for once, he called me by my actual name.

"Why not?" My voice strained a little.

I should've made him stop touching me.

I should've told him to step away.

But for whatever reason, I couldn't.

Maybe it was the hunger, or the bond, or the lure, but I just couldn't.

"They're not related in the slightest. One can't trigger the other." His grip eased up on my hips.

"Are you going to teach me how to feed?" My voice was barely above a whisper.

"You won't need a teacher. Turn around."

Letting out a soft breath, I released the countertop and did as he'd said. The front of my body brushed his as I did, and warmth blossomed in my middle at the touch. My hands landed on his chest, and the feel of his body beneath my palms made my face flush.

A hint of smoke danced over my skin, and he breathed in deeply, his eyes slamming shut. I didn't feel anything as that smoke slipped into his nostrils. It didn't disappear as he stole it, seeming unaffected by him. His chest rumbled against mine, the feeling and sound so soft I almost wanted to call it a purr. "You taste fucking incredible."

The reddish smoke on his skin was so bright it almost matched his glowing eyes—and it was starting to lean toward me, like I was a magnet or something. My hunger sharpened, and I fought an invisible battle with the fierce desire for the lust on his skin. Forcing my breathing to remain shallow, I didn't let myself have what I wanted.

It didn't make any sense to me.

None of it made any sense to me.

I didn't want to deal with it, and I couldn't—

"Take what you need from me, Tatum. You are in control." Rafael's voice rang with authority.

I didn't want to listen to him, but there was no alternative.

I needed what he offered, so I would have to take it.

My fingers dug into his chest as I stopped fighting myself. Sucking in a deep breath, I watched the smoke on his skin rush toward me.

The taste of it flooded my mouth and nose as I drank.

And drank.

And drank.

My body flushed, but parts of me I hadn't realized were tense began to relax.

He was exactly what I needed.

Lust was exactly what I needed.

My breathing remained deep and even as I took in more and more of his lust. As fast as I drank it, it continued dancing over his skin, his hands still firmly on my hips.

The unnatural hunger I'd felt eased slowly, until I was so full, I thought I might combust.

I pushed lightly at his chest, and he stepped away immediately. My breaths grew faster as I recovered from the experience, my head spinning and my body practically buzzing with the emotions I'd stolen.

"Holy shit," I mumbled, my eyes closing. My hand lifted to my chest, and I felt my heart pounding quickly beneath my palm.

"I told you it wouldn't kill you to relax, Tater-tot."

When I opened my eyes, I found his hands in the pockets of his joggers. His eyes still glowed a vibrant red, and the front of his pants were massively tented, but his lips were curved upward slightly.

The lure was gone, I supposed.

"You didn't tell me it would feel *good*," I said. He knew I was talking about the feeding.

The curve of his lips grew slightly. "I thought it was implied. We drink lust, not acid."

That was a fair point.

"Your demon form is beautiful." His hands remained in his pockets, but my forehead furrowed.

"My *what*?"

"Demons have two forms, like shifters. We shift when we lose control, and when we drink large amounts of lust. We can shift on command as well, but it tends to bring out our baser thoughts, actions, and desires, so we avoid it as much as possible. We're faster and stronger in that form, so it can be useful on occasion."

When fighting vampires, he meant.

"Show me," I commanded.

"If I shift on purpose, I won't be able to stop myself from touching you."

Shit.

Right.

We weren't together.

"Feed from me, then."

"You would need to use a vibrator, or slip a hand between your thighs."

The lust.

I wasn't lusty.

Dammit.

My curiosity mixed with the peaceful feeling I had, like everything was exactly the way it was supposed to be, and I decided I didn't care if it was awkward.

I wanted to see him shift. I wanted to know what demons looked like in their supernatural form.

"Did you buy a vibrator?"

"I did." He tilted his head toward the front door, where Sebastian had dropped that big box.

"Go get it, then."

He grinned. "You're sexy when you're bossy."

"Don't make me regret this."

He chuckled. "I'll do my best." After crossing the kitchen and pulling a box open, he came back with a simple, black, cylindrical vibrator. I'd had a vibrator before, so I did know a little about them, and knew it was made just to target my clit.

Honestly, I appreciated that he'd picked a simple one. I doubted I'd have the balls to stick something inside myself while he drank my lust.

He stepped back in front of me, and pressed the tip of the vibrator against me lightly, over my clothes. It was still turned off, but I sucked in a breath at the light pressure of the touch anyway.

It had been a long time since I'd had an orgasm.

Too long, clearly.

I was pretty damn proficient at ignoring my needs, though.

"Can I?" His voice was low and silky again.

"Only this time. And don't touch my skin."

His eyes burned redder, and he slowly increased the pressure to my clit.

It was nothing.

Almost nothing.

Barely anything.

But my breathing picked up anyway.

"Touch me, if you want to." His voice was still low, and there was no expectation in it.

I forced myself to grip the edge of the counter when my hands started moving toward his body. There was lust curling off of me, and it had color. Just a little color, but color.

We still weren't really together.

He had still been a dick.

I—

"Ohhh." I groaned when he turned the vibrator on, clutching the stone like a lifeline as he held it lightly against my center. The smoke around me swelled thicker, coming to life in red-hot waves.

Rafael inhaled, and I swear, his body *lit up*.

The lust around him glowed the brightest red I'd ever seen it, and his body shimmered.

I cried out as he pressed the vibrator against me a little harder, but I was so sensitive, he pushed me over the edge just like that.

His body transformed completely as he drank in my lust, holding one hand on my hip to balance me while I shattered.

I sucked in air, coming down from the high and taking in his demon form, both blissed-out and transfixed at the same time.

He was the same, but bigger.

Rougher.

Deadlier.

More powerful.

He'd grown a few inches taller, and his body had thickened, *everywhere*. His skin was covered in moving, curling magical markings that stretched over every visible inch of him, including his neck and face. Thick, ridged horns jutted from his head, and feathered wings spread behind him.

"Shit," I breathed, still panting. "Can I touch your wings?"

He had eased the vibrator away from me, giving me time to recover, and I assumed we were done. I was so relaxed, I was pretty sure I could've curled up on his couch and fallen asleep in minutes. The sun was still setting, but the time wouldn't faze me.

"If you're going to let me fuck you," he purred.

His voice was even sexier in that form, somehow.

Something whipped to the side a little behind him, and my eyes widened when I found a pointed tail.

"Maybe next time," I said, trying to ease myself away from him.

He pressed the vibrator back to my clit, and I nearly choked on my own spit. My hands caught his arm, and his chest rumbled with that same damn purr. "We're not done, mate."

Hot damn, what had I started?

"We're not?" I managed, my hips moving lightly in response to the vibration.

"Look at your body move for me, Tater-tot. You want more."

"Go to hell," I panted, my nails digging into his skin.

"Believe me, I've been there." His thumb dragged over my hip, and he took in another deep breath, thick with my lust. "No one has ever tasted like you. Give me more."

"I don't think I could stop myself if I wanted to."

His chest rumbled again, with satisfaction this time as he pressed the vibrator against me harder. "Your body knows its mate."

"My body knows it hasn't climaxed in ages," I gritted back.

"That's already changed." He took another lungful of my lust, and his wings spread open wide behind him. They were so much bigger than I expected, and my eyes fixed on them.

I didn't know why I wanted to touch them so badly, but I did.

I really, really did.

My fingers reached for them as my hips rocked, and he caught my wrist just before I touched him. "You touch my wings, you take your clothes off," he warned, that same damn purr in his voice.

The orgasm hit me, *hard.*

I cried out, bucking against the vibrator as he held me pinned against the cabinets.

My moan echoed through the massive apartment as I came down from the high, my fingers curled and my entire body alive with pleasure.

Rafael took my lust in, breath by breath, as he held the vibrator away from me. Relaxation set in—followed by common sense.

There was a stranger in front of me.

A stranger, who was a demon.

With wings.

Massive, gorgeous, *red* wings.

And horns.

And a tail.

And he was my husband.

Holy shit, what had I gotten myself into?

six

TATUM

"I THINK that's enough for now," I managed to say, taking the sleek black device from Rafael with a shaky hand.

I wanted more, as insane as it was to admit that.

My lust would fade eventually, though I had a terrible feeling it wasn't going to get anywhere near the cardboard-box state it had been in when we first met.

My finger struggled to find the button to turn it off, but I finally managed.

Rafe was still taking my lust in, drinking slowly and deeply. I could see the lust as it filled him, his wings still spread wide and proud, and his tail moving in smooth, rhythmic motions.

Finally, my lust started to abate.

Slowly, his inhales grew shallower.

His body finally shimmered again, and he shrank back to his human form.

Human*ish* form.

If I looked closely enough, I swore I could still see those magical tattoos moving over his skin, and the outline of those gorgeous wings behind him.

He eventually opened his eyes, and I found soft, clear blue irises staring at me.

His lips curved upward, his smile so much quicker and easier than it had been when his eyes were glowing. “Thank you, Tatum.”

“Uh... you’re welcome?”

He chuckled, the sound so smooth and gorgeous it gave me goosebumps. “Go sit down. I’ll finish dinner.”

His instruction caught me so off-guard that I didn’t even question it. My feet carried me across the room, and I sat down, pulling my phone from my pocket. My panties were so wet I was uncomfortable, but I wasn’t about to admit that to Rafael.

The silence was actually kind of peaceful as I checked my phone.

That peace faded as I saw the texts and missed calls. Most were from Miley and Brynn, and one was from Sebastian. I checked the text from Sebastian first, figuring it would take longer to reply to Miles and Brynn.

My eyebrows lifted when I read the message—it was a quick explanation about what happened to demons when they let themselves starve.

Apparently, their organs started turning to stone, like a vampire’s did. Rafael was in serious pain when he was starving, and not just hunger pains.

Shit.

But I had just fed Rafael, so that wasn't going to be a problem for us.

After sending him a thumbs up, I called Miles, knowing she'd put me on speaker so Brynn could hear. Miley was the mama bear out of the three of us, so it was just easier to work through her.

She answered the phone with a demanding, "You're still alive?"

I glanced at the kitchen, and my gaze met Rafael's for a moment. His lips curved upward playfully with the contact, and I looked away quickly. "For the most part."

"You can't answer sarcastically when you're imprisoned by your demon mate," Miley snapped.

"I'm not technically imprisoned." I paused, and then looked back at Rafe. "I'm not a prisoner, am I?"

"No. I'd have to follow you if you left, but I would never trap you here." His smile was gone, his forehead furrowing as he frowned.

Right.

He'd just gotten out of prison, and I'd just given him a shitty reminder.

Also... I was supposed to be convincing myself that he was a murderer. When had I forgotten that bit?

Clearly, it wasn't working.

My curiosity and newfound demonic magic were officially making me insane.

"Not a prisoner. I just checked," I said into the phone, looking away from Rafael again. My gaze moved over the stunning view of the mountains outside our windows. The sun was almost entirely behind them, leaving just a slice of light over the jagged outline of the range.

"How are the brothers? Hot?" Brynn put in.

"Extremely."

"What were they there for?"

"They brought groceries, and a new phone and computer for Rafe. And they made us dinner."

"Seriously?" Brynn asked

"Yep."

"So they're like normal brothers?" She sounded amused.

"My brother has never brought me any kind of food, so I'm going to go with no. They seem nice, though." I brushed a few damp strands of hair out of my eyes. "I saw your texts. What happened?"

"Someone literally bought out *all* of the candy from all three of our shops," Miley said. Her voice was as tense as I would've expected. "We were going to leave you alone so you had time to figure things out with your demon, but that's obviously off the table. Sophie resorted to selling your last test batch of peppermint truffles when your afternoon regulars came looking."

I sat up abruptly. "She did *not*."

"She did."

"I'm going to kill her."

"Oh, she knows."

I closed my eyes. "Dammit. This is why we should keep extra stocked in the freezer."

"You're the one who said they don't thaw perfectly," Brynn reminded me. "It's not a big deal, and none of us will complain about the extra money. That was a lot of candy. We'll stay up all night to get most of the basics remade, but you know the seasonal stuff is a little beyond our skill level."

"And the seasonal stuff sells like hotcakes," Miles added. "My baristas are *killer* at convincing people to take a pumpkin spice latte for now, and a pumkin spice truffle for later."

"I know. Mine are too." I collapsed back against the couch, and my gaze scanned the boxes on the table. I knew exactly who had bought out all three shops—but knowing that didn't do us any good. It wasn't like I could take them back and resell them.

Honestly, I should've told him from the beginning that I was the owner so he didn't do anything ridiculous.

Like buying three shops' worth of fancy candy.

"It's fine. You're right about the money. I'll drag Rafael back to the shop with me and spend the night working there while you guys go to town in the apartment."

"Perfect," Brynn said. "What should we prioritize?"

"I have spreadsheets of which products have sold the best in each of our shops over the last month. I'll check it and text the list out so you know what to work on too, Tatum."

"Sounds good. I should probably mention, I learned today that demons eat candy to stave off their hunger."

There was a long pause, until Brynn finally laughed. "Your new husband and his brothers bought out the candy at all *three* of our shops?"

"How can he handle that much candy? He's ridiculously muscular," Miley grumbled.

"And ridiculously rich, apparently," Brynn said.

"I don't think what they eat affects their appearances." I looked up at Rafael again, and he dipped his head, confirming my suspicions.

"Damn. Can you ask one of the brothers to come into my shop and mate me up?" Brynn teased.

Miley snorted, and I grinned. "I'll give it a go."

"We'll send the list over in the next few minutes. Good luck convincing your demon to spend the night baking with you," Miley said.

"I'll probably need it, so thanks. Talk later."

We hung up, and I looked over at Rafael. I found him on his phone, his forehead wrinkled as he scrolled.

His gaze lifted to mine after a moment. "Your half of that conversation was interesting, Tater-tot."

Obviously, I was going to have to come clean.

"A little search brought me to your shop's social media page," he said, his eyes narrowing slightly. "You're not a barista."

Yeah, I probably should've told him earlier.

"I am, actually. During the busy stretches, at least."

"According to this picture, you're the genius behind all of the *Coffee & Toffee* recipes. And one of the shops' owners. Your best friends own the other two locations."

There it was.

"I never told you I was *only* a barista."

"You never told me you were the candy chef I was raving about, either." He continued staring at me, his eyes still narrowed. "You should've clarified."

"You didn't seem interested in learning the truth."

"I will always be interested in the truth when it comes to you." There was a growl to his voice that I liked tremendously.

"Good. The truth is, I have to go back to the shop and spend all night cooking. Miley and Brynn can handle most of the recipes, but the more complex candies have too many components. They're also most of our best-sellers, so there's no way around going in tonight. How far apart can we be before there are negative effects? And what happens when those effects set in, exactly?"

"The effects are unique to the individual. Most people report obsessive thoughts and paranoia about their mate. It's more of a drive to get back to their side than full-on psychosis."

Well, that still sounded crappy to me.

Rafael added, "I don't know how far apart we can be without setting it off, but it's not worth testing right now. My hunger is sated for the moment, but it will take time for my body to reach equilibrium. We can't do anything to set my magic off any more than it already is."

That was fair.

And he wasn't putting up a fight about me running the shop, which seemed like a good sign.

"Alright, you can help me," I said. "But I am *very* particular. If you can't follow directions, I'll make you sit at the tables, as far from the kitchen as possible."

He gave me an amused grin. "I'll be the best assistant you've ever had."

"Don't push it."

He chuckled, and I fought a smile.

RAFAEL FILLED our bowls with the pasta his brother had made, then quickly stored the rest in the fridge before we headed out. He seemed to be in a much better mood than he had been before he fed from me, and I couldn't say I minded it.

I could—and *did*—ignore the soft smoke that danced lightly over my skin, though. And the vibrant red of Rafael's, too.

He didn't get off when we fed from each other, which hadn't passed my notice. He had yet to bring it up, and I sure as hell wasn't going to.

The food was hot and smelled incredible, so when he asked for my keys, I reluctantly handed them over after making sure he had a license.

He did.

I GORGED myself on the best pasta I'd had in years while he drove. My music played from the car's sound system, filling the air with the laid-back pop I preferred. Neither of us said anything, but it wasn't awkward.

Just relaxed.

Miley texted the list into our group chat, and I looked over it to make sure I'd been right about what I needed to remake.

I was.

It felt nice to be right about what my customers wanted, but there was a very solid amount of work to do. I was up for the challenge, but I probably wouldn't finish until around the time the shop opened.

RAFAEL FOUND my shop without any navigational help on my part, parking in my usual spot without pause. Sophie would've finished closing up an hour earlier. So, as I expected, the shop was empty and dark when we stepped inside.

"It smells incredible in here," Rafael remarked, taking everything in with much more interest than he had the first time he was there. Whether that was because he had been starving, or because he hadn't known I owned it, I wasn't sure.

"Always does," I agreed, setting my stuff down. He took a seat in our small break room, starting on his pasta while I tied my apron on. "Do you drink coffee?"

"I used to."

Something told me the *used to* translated to *before prison*.

"What's your favorite?"

"Whatever tastes the least like coffee." He flashed me a playful grin, and my lips curved upward.

Honestly, that didn't surprise me at all.

I made him a pumpkin spice latte, since they were the most popular at the moment, and left him with it while he ate. He looked surprised when he accepted it, and thanked me twice before I got started.

With music playing loud enough to silence my thoughts, I focused on what I was doing and worked quickly. Rafael joined me as soon as his food was gone, and when I gave him the easiest jobs (and watched him like a hawk until I was sure he could handle them), he didn't complain at all.

His shoulders were relaxed, and his movements smoother than they had been when we first met.

Clearly, feeding him had helped. I could hardly believe the upbeat man was the same red-eyed demon who'd stepped into the shop and told me I was his. Admitting that seemed unnecessary, so I stayed quiet.

We worked without problem, only talking when we had to, but the atmosphere was as calm as it only got when I was in the kitchen alone. That was a little bizarre to me, but I liked it tremendously.

I taught Rafael how to make a few of our most popular drinks whenever we had a minute to spare, or started getting tired. When he realized I was only teaching him the sugary ones I knew he would like, he made me teach him my favorite drinks, too.

We finally left the shop as Sophie arrived to open up.

I pointed a finger at her, my eyes drooping despite the caffeine pumping through my veins. "I have to kill you for giving away my test truffles."

She lifted her hands, but flashed me a grin. Though her gaze flicked to Rafael a few times, she didn't question his presence. "You know how Jen and Ian are about their truffles. I had no choice but to break them out. Other customers arrived during the process, and I couldn't turn them down when they were so intrigued. I did tell everyone they were still a work in progress, for the record, and charged them extra for the experience."

"You're lucky I'm exhausted," I grumbled at her.

"Yep. And you're lucky I'm so damn good." She winked at me.

"I know I am." I couldn't fight a grin, and looked at Rafael. "Ready?"

"Yup." He offered me an arm, and I dutifully set my hand in the crook of his elbow.

We made it back to my car quickly, and when he took the driver's seat, I didn't even consider protesting. The exhaustion was strong with me.

After stops at Brynn and Miley's shops to deliver the desserts —they were on their way to mine when I texted them—we finally drove back to Rafael's place.

When we got inside, he pointed out the spare bed. I didn't make a peep before stripping out of my bra and his pants.

Collapsing on the ridiculously-comfortable mattress, I pulled the luxurious sheets to my chin, and promptly fell asleep.

seven

TATUM

I EXPECTED to sleep like a rock after everything that had happened, but as soon as I drifted off, the dreams began.

I'd never been someone who had sex dreams. They just weren't something I'd ever had to deal with.

But whew, the dreams were *filthy*.

Full of Rafael's bare, demonic body. His smile was wicked and his tattoos danced as he devoured me, touched me, and fucked me in every way there was. The dreams always changed before I could climax, driving me to near insanity, yet holding me captive in sleep anyway.

They were unreal.

Absolutely unreal.

And even more unreal was the fact that I actually enjoyed them.

• • •

IT WAS late in the evening by the time I finally woke up, feeling incredibly off-balance. I was slicker between my thighs than I could remember ever being, and my body both ached and throbbed, desperately needing release.

I could hear someone cooking in the kitchen, and the low murmur of male voices. Pulling Rafael's t-shirt over my head, I stumbled to the bathroom and used the facilities, hoping it would ease the tension in my middle.

It helped a tiny bit, but that was all.

Staring at myself in the mirror, I blinked once.

And again.

I still looked the same. Same light green eyes, same cinnamon hair, same dusting of freckles. But I was different, too. My skin was clearer, and my usual redness was gone.

Turning my head side to side, I mused about the differences. They were small, but significant enough that I noticed them.

Rafael's magic had changed me in more ways than the obvious bit where I needed to drink his emotions. According to him, I could shift into a demon form, too.

Whether or not I wanted to see it was still up in the air. Shifting into a monster with horns, wings, and a tail was definitely outside my comfort zone.

I'd survive, though. I always did.

I slipped out of the bathroom, hesitating at the top of the stairs as I tried to hear part of the conversation. My stomach was still tense, and I didn't have a clean pair of panties to change into, so I was still annoyingly wet.

"She sent invitations out today," one of Rafael's brothers said, his voice faint with the distance between us. "You need to talk to Tatum about it. Mom personally called and invited her parents, and they had no idea about the bond."

"We have two months to figure it out. We'll be fine," Rafael said, his voice not nearly as smooth as it had been during the night.

What party was he talking about?

And what the hell? His mom had called my parents?

I padded back into my room, looking for my phone, but couldn't find it. I had to have left it in my bag the night before.

Or earlier that morning, I guess. I'd charged it at the coffee shop, so I knew it wasn't dead.

"You talked to her about the dreams, at least?" one of his brothers asked.

"Didn't get to it," Rafael admitted.

My face flushed at the reminder about the hot dreams.

I wanted to climb back in bed and pull the blankets over my head until life magically went back to normal, but obviously that wouldn't help at all. If I wanted things to change, I was going to have to change them myself.

"You need this woman to like you," one of the brothers put in.

"I'm working on it."

I figured that was as good a time as any to interject myself into the awkward conversation, and padded down the stairs.

When three sets of eyes landed on me, and lingered, I looked down.

Shit.

I'd forgotten to put his pants and my bra back on.

And his shirt was still tied up at my hip, showing off my black lace underwear.

Awkward.

Hopefully they couldn't visibly see how horny I was.

Rafe's eyes were red again, and the smoky lust around him grew thicker and more vibrant.

They'd already seen enough of me. So, I went ahead and gave them all a small wave before I grabbed my purse off the table, then walked back up the stairs.

"Look at my mate's ass, and I will fucking castrate you," Rafael growled. His feet were heavy on the stairs behind me, and he caught my hand as I stepped around the corner that led to my room. It didn't even have its own door—everything was wide open.

Too open, clearly.

With a light tug, he pulled me back. I stumbled a little, and he caught me with a firm hand on my hip.

I sucked in a breath at the massive presence of him. I'd forgotten how big he was, and the dreams had screwed with my mind. Reeling a bit, I tried to reign myself in. "What's up?"

Did that sound cool?

Did people even say "what's up" anymore?

I had no idea.

It took effort not to cringe.

“What are you doing?” The red in his eyes brought my mind back to his demonic form, and my toes curled.

I needed help. Serious help.

Was there such a thing as an intervention for women who accidentally ended up mated to a demon? I had to google that.

“Needed my phone.” I lifted my purse as evidence.

“Where are your clothes?”

I would’ve expected him to ask me to strip more, not to tell me to cover up.

“I forgot to put them on, clearly.” I forced myself to stand up straighter. It wasn’t like I’d tried to put on a show for his brothers; I legitimately forgot to get dressed. “It was a long night.”

“Clearly. You’re dripping in lust, Tater-tot.” He squeezed my hip lightly. “I forgot to warn you about the dreams.”

“What dreams?” I answered too quickly, my face flushing.

I really wasn’t a kinky or lusty person in most situations. I hadn’t had sex with a guy in... two years? Three? Not since I’d been out of culinary school. It had just seemed like so much effort, and the payoff wasn’t worth it.

“Hungry demons unconsciously project their desires to the people around them while they sleep.”

“Oh. *Those* dreams.”

There was a flicker of heat in his eyes. "Yes. I can see my magic got you worked up."

"No comment." I brushed hair out of my eyes.

His eyes gleamed wickedly. "I put a vibrator in the bathroom, and one in both of our nightstands. Just in case."

"Just in case I climb into your bed by accident while horny?" I drawled.

He grinned. "Exactly. If I'm not already up here, let me know that you're going to use it and I'll stick around and feed."

Because that wasn't awkward at all.

"What party are you talking about?" I gestured to the stairs, in the general direction of his brothers.

"It's traditional for a demon to throw a large celebration after he or she takes a mate. My mother has taken it upon herself to throw ours. We typically stay at a resort someone owns, and spend a whole weekend drinking and dancing."

My eyebrows shot upward. "And your mom managed to find my parents and invite them to *that*?"

"Unfortunately." He ran a hand through his waves. "I called her while you were asleep and tried to talk her down, but had no luck. She thinks prison addled my brain."

"It did," I pointed out.

"She doesn't need to know that."

I let out a puff of air. "I'm not close with my family, Rafe."

"This is the demon version of a wedding. The female usually wears a white gown every day. Not inviting another demon's family would be a grave insult."

"I'm not a demon," I pointed out. "Or I wasn't, until yesterday."

"Even if you hadn't changed, your family would still be invited. It's tradition."

I huffed. "Tradition is ridiculous."

"Often, yes." His lips curved upward slightly. "But it keeps us together, so we all play along. It's been a decade since the last mating party, so there will be a lot of enthusiasm about our bond."

I wasn't good with crowds, and I had a hard time lying to anyone, let alone my family.

"My parents are not easy people to get along with," I finally said. "They're going to be difficult about this."

"I'll win them over." His hand brushed my bare hip lightly, and I shuddered.

Images from my dreams rippled to life in my mind. "How do we stop the dreams?"

"My magic will settle as I continue to heal."

"You need to drink from me to do that," I pointed out, still ignoring the wetness between my thighs and the red in my cheeks.

"I do." His hand brushed my hip again, and I stepped back.

He let me go.

"I need to do damage control with my parents, and check in with Sophie and Miley. Your brothers are probably waiting for you."

He dipped his head.

"The government can't find out that we formed a mate bond just to keep me out of prison. That includes my mother, and just to be safe, your family too. Tell them we're in love. If they ask for stories, make them vague."

I jerked my head in a nod.

His gaze lingered on my face for a long moment before he finally left me in my room alone.

I let out a long breath, dropping my purse on the foot of the bed so I could find my phone quickly. It was vibrating when I picked it up, and I couldn't stop myself from grimacing when I saw my mom's old face smiling back from the screen. She hadn't looked like that since her last three surgeries.

Avoiding her wasn't going to do me any good, so I hit the button and lifted the phone to my ear. "Hey, mom."

"Why is a member of the supernatural government calling me to say my daughter is married to her son?" Her voice was so loud, I had to jerk the phone away from my ear. I could still hear fine with it six inches away from my face.

Our situation seemed to get messier by the hour.

"I'm doing great, thanks for asking. How are you?"

"Tatum Renee, this is not the time for jokes! What kind of supernatural is he? Why haven't you told me anything about him? Why didn't I get an invitation to the wedding?!"

"Easy, mom. He's a good guy, and that's what matters." I closed my eyes, leaning against the wall.

Ultimately, I *did* believe it was true.

As much as I was trying to convince myself that he was dangerous, I knew the difference between taking out vampires who were killing humans, and murdering someone in cold blood.

And I always tried to lie as little as possible. Lying wasn't one of my talents on a good day, and it wasn't a good day. The ache in my lower belly hadn't dissipated any more than the obnoxious dampness in my panties. I needed to have a conversation with Rafael about where we were going to live, and with my roommates about me possibly moving out, and...

Yeah.

It was a lot.

"Tatum." This time, her voice was a threat.

"His name is Rafael. We met at the coffee shop. He came in one day, and we hit it off. I was going to call you today, now that we've made it official, but it seems like his mom went crazy planning the mating party and beat me to it."

I went on, "I'm sorry you didn't hear it from me personally, but this is a good thing for us. Rafael needs me, and I need him. We fit well together." I tried to throw as much truth in there as I could, so there was a better chance she would buy it.

Honestly, it wasn't a huge stretch to think I wouldn't tell them. If I did start dating someone, I would definitely keep it to myself until I was positive it was going to become permanent.

Dating was off the table, though.

Hell, *everyone* was off the table except Rafe, and I didn't even know how to feel about that. The emotions were too tangled, and too messy.

My mom was silent for a moment.

A long, long moment.

"It hurts that you didn't trust me enough to tell me," she finally said, her voice much quieter.

"I know, mom. I'm sorry."

"You're not even having a ceremony?"

I hadn't had time to consider a wedding, but she was obsessed with big parties and social events. If she didn't have a wedding to invite her friends to, or at least just brag about and show pictures of, she'd be pissed. And heartbroken.

Mostly pissed, though.

She was always concerned about appearances.

Which meant I had to have a wedding, or listen to her complain about the fact that I hadn't for the rest of my life. Option A was the clear winner.

"Rafael's mom took over all the planning in a matter of hours. I'm glad she did—you know I wouldn't enjoy throwing a huge party—but we haven't really had time to talk about whether we want to do a wedding ceremony while we're there. I think it might help me transition better, so I'm leaning toward doing it."

"I would like to see you married, if you're living together in a permanent bond the way supernatural beings do," my mom said, sniffling a little. "And I would've thrown the party for you."

"I'll talk to Rafe about it. I'm sure he'll agree to a wedding. He'll pay for your plane tickets too, if you're planning on coming."

It seemed like the least he could do, and I knew they'd complain about the money, even though they had *plenty*.

"Anastasia already paid for them as a gift," my mom said, sniffling again. I assumed that was his mom's name, but couldn't act like I didn't know it. "Tell him to spend the money on your dress, instead."

"I will. I love you, mom."

"I love you too. I'm glad you're happy, Tatum."

"Thank you. See you soon." I hung up the phone and leaned harder against the wall.

The front door opened and closed, and I heard footsteps on the stairs a moment later. I looked over at the doorway, not surprised to find Rafael standing there with his hands in the pockets of his joggers.

"We have to do a wedding ceremony while we're there," I told him. "White dress, flowers, cake, and all."

"No problem." His voice was gentler than I expected.

"I don't even know if they can get a dress done in time. Or any of the other stuff."

"You'll need four dresses, actually. Only one will be white. I called a place in town earlier, and they said they'll make it happen."

"Four wedding dresses seems excessive." I wiped away a few tears.

"Pretty much everything about demons is excessive, Tater-tot. I thought you realized that when you saw my wings, horns, and tail." His lips curved upward, and I choked on a laugh. "I set up an appointment for you tomorrow evening. I figured we need to decide what to do about the living situation tonight."

"And the food situation, since your eyes are glowing again."

He dipped his head. "I'll need to feed a lot more than usual over the next few weeks."

"It's fine. We'll figure it out."

"Of course." He stepped closer to me and carefully slipped an arm around my waist. Though part of me wanted to protest or move away, I found myself leaning against him. "I'm sorry you had to lie to her."

"I need you to promise me you won't ask me to lie for you again, after everything has settled down with the mating," I told him, honesty ringing in my voice.

"I promise." His second arm met the first around my back, and I leaned closer to him, my eyes closing again. Maybe I shouldn't have accepted the support he offered, but I just couldn't stop myself.

One thing I'd said to my mom had been completely true.

We needed each other.

TATUM

AS WE HEADED down the stairs, Rafael explained that Sebastian and Zander had shown up to cook for us again after he told them we'd been up all night working. According to him, they really just wanted the boxes of candy they'd left behind the day before, and I snorted.

I didn't know if he was right, but there were significantly fewer boxes when we reached the bottom of the stairs.

And, there was a massive bouquet of flowers sitting on the table. Red roses—clearly for or from someone with romantic feelings.

"Who are the flowers for?" I asked him, eyeing the vase suspiciously. "You flipped out about the possibility of me having a boyfriend, so you better not be dating some demon chick."

He laughed, and the noise echoed through the apartment. "Demons don't *date*. We fuck from time to time, but that's the extent of it. I bought the flowers to go with your gift."

"What gift?"

"The vibrators, Tater-tot."

Oh.

Right.

"It doesn't count as a gift when you buy it for yourself." I ducked out from beneath his arm, deciding I needed space from him before I got even hornier than I already was. My abdomen was still crampy.

"I was going to buy you a ring too, but I didn't know what you'd want."

"That's kind of a requirement, since we want people to think this is real." I gestured between us.

His eyes narrowed slightly as he watched me stroll up to the casserole dish on the counter and pluck a few steaming, sauce-covered vegetables off the top with my fingers. "This *is* real."

I rolled my eyes at him. "You mated with me so you wouldn't have to spend your life in prison."

"I mated with you because we were potential mates, and I would rather spend an immortal life with my potential mate than die in prison."

"Exactly. What we have isn't love, dedication, or attachment. It's fake." I grabbed the serving spoon that had been left beside the dish, and cut into the casserole. It was a little crazy for me to think that rich demons cooked casseroles for each other, but I guessed they had probably been alive a long time. Old habits died hard.

"The bond is real." He finally joined me in the kitchen, pulling bowls out of a cupboard. "There's no way to be more attached than we currently are. Love isn't the most important factor here."

"Not for you, clearly."

I accepted the bowl he handed me and plopped a huge chunk of the casserole in it. I was hungry, and not for lust.

"I'm sorry," he began.

"Stop apologizing, Rafael. We both know you're not really sorry. And even if you were, talk is cheap." I grabbed a spoon and headed for the stairs. "I still have to text Brynn and Miles about the shops. I'll let you know when I'm ready to figure out the living situation."

He didn't say another word as I climbed the stairs, my chest hollow.

Back in my room—or my chunk of the upstairs, since it wasn't entirely separate from the rest of the apartment—I sat down on the edge of the bed and squeezed my eyes shut against an onslaught of emotion.

I had never fallen in love with anyone.

I'd never been so obsessed with a guy that I wanted to move in with him or tie my life to his.

I'd never experienced passion like that.

And now, I would never have that chance.

Rafael had done more than just tie us together; he had stolen my future from me.

I needed to start looking at him and thinking about him in those terms, somehow.

I couldn't let myself think of him and his brothers as attractive demons who cooked dinner for each other, and gorged themselves on chocolate to curb their hunger. It made them seem too human.

And when they seemed human, I let myself like them too much.

I wasn't entirely sure how to balance everything in my mind, though. I wasn't someone who couldn't survive without a plan and a spreadsheet, like Miles was, but I liked stability. I felt better when I knew what was coming and how I was going to face it.

But I had no idea what to do about my demon problem.

A few tears leaked from my eyes as I ate, wrapping my mind around the fact that this was my future. *Rafael* was my future.

And I could either hate it for the rest of my life—my potentially immortal life—or I could do my best to adapt.

Adapt or die, right?

Death was starting to sound a little easier, but I wasn't ready to let go yet.

So I was going to have to keep adapting, no matter how much it sucked.

WHEN I HEADED BACK down the stairs, Rafe was sitting on the couch with his empty bowl beside him. His attention was trained on the windows, and he didn't hear me behind him. Or at least, he didn't turn around if he did.

I rinsed my bowl and put it in the dishwasher before padding over to the couch and sitting down somewhat near him. He turned his gaze to me, and then physically turned the rest of himself so he could look at me face-to-face.

"How far apart can we be right now without causing the psychosis?" I asked.

He lifted a shoulder. "A mile or so at the most, I would guess."

Damn.

"Living in our own apartments are out, then. Even if they weren't, we need people to believe we're into each other. I imagine your government will be suspicious if we're living separately."

He nodded. "We'll have to stay together. I can buy a house in town if you'd be more comfortable that way; something near your shop would make life simpler."

Sharp pain cut through my chest. "I've been saving up to buy a house for a while, and have a long way to go. I have a hard time wrapping my mind around the fact that there are people wealthy enough to just go out and buy a home without batting an eye."

"We're used to different lifestyles."

"*Extremely* different."

He dipped his head. "As soon as we've filled out the paperwork to let the world know you're mine, the government will issue you an ID that marks us as mates. That gives you complete access to everything I own. You could walk into a bank, show your ID, and withdraw as much money as you wanted."

I blinked.

That was... different.

"I know some married humans keep separate accounts, but it's not done among supernaturals. Mates function as one in every way, including financially. Like I explained, no one takes a mate lightly."

I blinked again.

He was serious.

Not just about the money—though he seemed serious about that too.

He was serious that he considered our mate bond real, despite the way it had come to be.

I would need time to process the money bit, so I steered the conversation back to the housing situation. "I like your apartment, and the drive is only fifteen minutes. I think we should just live here until we have a real reason or desire to move."

His shoulders relaxed a bit. "That would be simplest."

I nodded. "We need to go back to my place tonight, though. I need my stuff."

"That's not a problem."

"Okay, now the eating bit. Just give it to me straight, Rafe. How often do you need to feed to recover?"

"Once a day will be fine," he said.

His grimace told me he wasn't giving me the honesty I'd requested, so I narrowed my eyes at him.

His grimace deepened. "Twice a day would be better for the next few days. I'll recover much faster, and then we could get down to two or three a week until I'm completely healthy again."

"That's the fastest way to stop the dreams?" I checked.

"The fastest way would be two to three feedings a day until my hunger abates, then once a day until I'm balanced again."

"We'll go with that. You need to feed before we go to my old apartment, right?"

"If your friends will be there, that would be better."

I rose to my feet, ignoring the way my heartbeat picked up and smoke tendrils began radiating from me again. "Let's get to it, then."

He caught my hand before I could walk away, and when our gazes met, his gaze was... hot. "There's one more thing to discuss, Tater-tot."

"There are probably a thousand more things to discuss," I countered. "We'll get to them when they come up."

"This one is too important to discuss later."

I had no idea what he was going to say, so I just waited.

His thumb brushed the backs of my knuckles. "As you know, I mated with you to stay out of prison. However, you seem to believe that's all I intend our bond to be."

I frowned. "What do you mean?"

"You see our mating as fake," he said, his eyes locked with mine. "Obviously, I haven't made myself clear enough."

My frown deepened, my forehead wrinkling.

"This is the beginning of our forever. I will win your heart, and give you mine as well."

It took a moment, but I processed what he was saying.

He didn't think love was unimportant. He thought it would grow between us over time. In his mind, he hadn't stolen my future; he was just getting started at giving me one.

"You expect us to care about each other and function as actual mates?" I asked him, my heart still beating a little faster.

"I expect to flirt, spoil, and fuck my way into your life until neither of us has an ounce of desire to live apart again."

Shit.

"What do you expect me to say to that?" I finally asked.

His lips curved upward slightly. "How about a good old, 'go ahead and try,' or 'good luck with that'?"

I huffed out a laugh. "You're obnoxious."

"So I've been told." He lifted my hand to his lips and brushed a kiss to my knuckles. The gesture was both soft and playful, and despite the red glow, his gaze was the same. "Are you going to let me use the vibrator on you again?"

I hadn't even thought about it, but I answered quickly.

"No. After that last announcement, I'm thinking a little space would be best. You can feed from another room, right?"

"I can." He answered easily.

Too easily.

I narrowed my eyes at him. "I'm not here for half-truths, Rafael."

"It will take longer to sate me if there's more distance between us."

"Alright, you can come to my room with me." I paused for a heartbeat, imagining having him in my bed with me, and then corrected myself. "Maybe the couch would be safer, to keep things more appropriate."

He chuckled. "There's nothing appropriate about feeding on lust, Tater-tot."

"I need a shitty name for you too," I grumbled, as he stood.

Somehow, I'd already forgotten how he towered over me with all those gorgeous muscles.

My body warmed, and the damn smoke on my skin thickened.

"Call me whatever you want. You'll be more comfortable in my bed, so we'll keep the feedings there. Then, you don't have to think about feeding me every time you curl up in yours."

My face flushed. "How did you know I was thinking about that?"

"Your face gives everything away." His fingertip brushed my nose, and then he towed me toward the stairs. "Do you know how difficult it is not to touch you when you walk around in nothing but your panties and my shirt, Tater-tot? I swear, you're trying to kill me." He looked back at me as we reached the steps, his eyes moving slowly down my figure.

I flushed hotter. "Do *not* try to distract me with lust. I should be trying to come up with a terrible nickname for you."

He chuckled, and we headed up. "Go ahead."

"Raffle. Raffy Taffy. Raft. Craft..." I trailed off, not coming up with anything for a minute as I wracked my brain for more words that had "raf" in them.

"Draft," Rafael offered.

I gave him a look. "You're helping me come up with a shitty nickname for you?"

He flashed me a grin. "I'm the one who refused to stop calling you by yours. Seems like due diligence at this point."

True.

That was fair.

"G*raff*iti," I threw out.

"Riffraff," he put in. We reached his bedroom, but I was too distracted by our conversation to care.

"Perfect. That's the one. If you call me Tater-tot, I'm calling your rich, gorgeous ass *Riffraff*."

He laughed. "Technically, your gorgeous ass is just as rich as mine now."

"We are not dealing in technicalities at this point, Riffraff." I held a finger up, and his grin widened. "And don't lie to me. I know I'm not anywhere near as attractive as you. Unlike you, I wasn't born to inspire lust in people." I plopped down on the edge of the bed, and he sat on the other side, tucking his legs beneath the blankets. I followed suit, only a bit reluctantly.

"Insult yourself again, and I'll have no choice but to prove you wrong," he said matter-of-factly. "You wouldn't have been my potential mate if I couldn't live the rest of my life content to look at no one but you. You are the most beautiful woman I've ever seen—and even when I wasn't hungry, you saw the lust dancing off my skin."

He wasn't wrong about that last bit. I'd noticed it a dozen times while we were at my coffee shop the night before. There was no avoiding the fact that the man was attracted to me.

"I don't know how you could possibly prove me wrong." I leaned over, opening the nightstand's drawer. Inside, I found another black vibrator—a different one than I'd used the last time.

It was shaped to go inside me and vibrate my clit at the same time.

My face flushed at the sight of it, but I grabbed it and lowered to the mattress on my back. "Where's the other one?"

"In the bathroom. I figured you might need a *hot* shower one of these mornings." He brushed a few strands of hair off my face, his touch feather-light. "Tell me your rules."

"No touching me." It was the only rule I needed. He had yet to push me on anything, even when he was feeding, so I didn't think he'd try something that could make me uncomfortable. If he did, I knew how to knee him in the balls.

Our experience in the kitchen had been enough to tell me he had a dirty mouth, and that I didn't mind it one bit. If I had to guess, that was the real reason he was asking for rules. He knew damn well I wasn't offering to have sex with him, after all. And if it went anything like it had the last time, he wouldn't even try to get himself off.

I slipped my panties off, and Rafael's hot gaze followed them to the floor. "Fuck, I love the idea of you naked in my bed."

"It's more than an idea right now, Riffraff." I turned the vibrator on, and hesitantly slipped it between my thighs, sucking in a breath at the feeling of the thick, cold plastic against my clit.

"If you want to touch me, I'm all yours," he said, rolling onto his side. There was a solid inch between his chest and my arm, but he was close.

My breath came out faster, and the tendrils of smoke around me reddened by the moment.

Rafael took a deep breath in, a growl rumbling his chest as he inhaled my lust. My gaze was on him as the transformation took over. His body swelled bigger and thicker, horns appearing on his head and gorgeous wings unfolding behind him. One spread over the mattress, so it didn't end up beneath him.

The magical markings rolled over his skin, and the glow in his eyes grew brighter. "I've never tasted lust as delicious as yours, mate. Move your hips for me. Chase the pleasure."

I didn't want to listen to him, but... I did.

My hips lifted, and a cry escaped me as the sensations grew more intense. I gripped the sheet as I fought to stop myself from reaching out and grabbing him. I wanted to feel his skin against mine, to anchor myself that way, but couldn't.

The lust around me thickened, and Rafael took in another deep breath. "You're close, Tatum. I can taste it. Let yourself lose control."

My hips jerked, and more cries escaped me as I finally went over the edge.

Tugging the vibrator away, I dropped my ass back to the mattress and panted. "Holy shit."

Rafe took in another deep breath of my lust. "You can do better than that."

I let go of the sheet long enough to smack him on the abdomen in response. Unfortunately for me, the man was wearing a shirt. He didn't grow quite enough to tear the fabric, so he wasn't about to be shirtless.

He took in another deep breath of my lust. "We're not finished."

"Are you always this needy?" I asked, opening my thighs just a tiny bit and bringing the vibrator back to my clit.

My eyes fluttered closed.

Damn, that felt good.

"Luckily for you, yes."

I snorted.

His chest rumbled. "Take the blanket off and let me watch you, Tater-tot." It wasn't a command—and even if it had been, he knew I wouldn't obey him without questioning.

A breathless laugh escaped me. "Not going to happen, Riffraff.

The idea was appealing, though.

Really, really appealing.

Lust swelled around me at the thought, and my body started moving again, just barely.

And once that thought was in my head, I couldn't get it out.

I finally huffed out a breath and threw my half of the blanket further down the bed, then grabbed Rafael's arm. He turned it in my grip, catching my hand in his and threading his fingers through mine.

His eyes devoured my bare lower half, and my hips jerked as he took another deep breath of my lust.

"Open your thighs," he growled.

I forced them open, one of my legs draping over Rafael's. His tail wrapped around my calf, the firm ridges along the length of it digging lightly into my skin.

"Give me the vibrator."

I didn't want to give in easily... but I wanted him to continue taking control.

So, I handed it over.

"No more touching," I warned, my chest still rising and falling quickly.

"I won't." Rafael dragged the tip of the vibrator over my clit before he found my entrance far too easily. Dipping it in my slickness, he eased it just an inch inside me. "You look so damn good like this. Open wide for me, dripping wet with the lust that tastes so fucking sweet."

My entire body froze as he slowly filled me with it. My breathing grew ragged, and I trembled.

He slid it out a little, and then back in.

My hips rocked along with it, and he continued to move it. "Shit," I breathed, as he hit a sensitive spot inside me. My hips jerked, and he repeated the motion, finding it perfectly.

"Let go, Tater-tot. Climax for me," he commanded.

The pleasure cut through me sharply, and I cried out. Rafael inhaled my lust again and again, drinking it in.

I moaned as I collapsed back on the bed. "Why are you so good at that? I don't even want to know how many times you've done this with someone else."

He chuckled, his voice low and rumbly. "Demons rarely have sex with humans. When we drink their lust, we take it away. And there are so few demons, we don't make it a habit to hook up with someone more than once a century or so." He took in another deep breath of my lust, and more replaced it just as fast. He was still holding the vibrator between my thighs, and letting me squeeze the shit out of his hand too.

Plus, his tail was wrapped around my leg.

I kind of liked that.

I blinked up at the ceiling, thinking back to the way he had affected Sophie, Hector, and Miley when he accidentally drank their emotions. They had gone neutral—it hadn't turned them on, and the emotions certainly hadn't come back right away. Sucking away someone's lust *would* make it difficult to have sex. "I didn't put that together."

"Many people don't." He inhaled again, and I watched the vibrant red smoke regenerate once more. "How often did you share a bed with someone, before you were mine?"

The way he phrased that almost made me smile.

Then again, the orgasms also helped on that front.

"Rarely. I had a boyfriend for a few months while I was in culinary school, so there was plenty of sex, but I didn't get off every time. Or even most of the time. I was trying to figure out how to break up with him when he broke up with me."

"You will never have that problem with me," he said, his tail tightening around my leg.

"I'm realizing that." I closed my eyes. "Damn, I feel good."

"I was right about relaxing, wasn't I?" He inhaled again. "You need this as much as I do."

"Maybe." I wasn't willing to admit aloud that he was right, but... well, he was.

His tail disappeared from around my leg, and I was a little disappointed when I looked over and found him in his human form. But those gorgeous blue eyes met mine, his lips curved upward in happiness or humor, and the disappointment vanished.

It should've been a crime to be that pretty.

Then again, Rafael clearly didn't need any help on the crime side of things.

He slipped the vibrator out of me and stepped into the bathroom connected to his portion of the floor long enough to wash it.

When he stepped into the room, he tucked it back in his nightstand. "Let's go get your things. You can feed me again tonight, afterward."

I eased myself to a sitting position, a little dazed from the orgasms. When he picked up my panties, the smoke around me thickened again as I watched him tuck them in his pocket.

"I need to wear those."

"They're drenched, Tater-tot. I'm keeping them as a trophy." The bastard winked at me.

"You don't need a trophy. You already tricked me into swearing myself to you for the rest of our immortal lives. Which, by the way, I have yet to wrap my mind around."

"Immortality is weird," he agreed. "And I'm keeping my trophy anyway." Opening one of his drawers, he pulled out a pair of clean boxer-briefs and tossed them to me.

After a moment, I gave up on fighting with him and pulled them on. They looked similar enough to biker shorts that I'd just untie his shirt and wear them like that.

"I feel like the fact that your underwear fit me should make me want to eat less chocolate," I remarked, untying the knot in my shirt.

"Don't be ridiculous. My hands are too big for your tight little ass as it is."

A laugh burst from me.

He was the ridiculous one... and I was starting to like that more than I could admit to him, or myself.

nine

TATUM

THE DRIVE to my apartment was peaceful, and I warned Brynn and Miley that we were on our way when we left, so they wouldn't be caught off-guard when we got there.

Brynn wasn't star-struck by him thankfully, and when Miley started questioning him, she joined in.

He had no problem answering their questions, his entire body at ease while he talked and helped me pack my shit into suitcases. And then into garbage bags, when I ran out of suitcases.

Even the garbage bags didn't faze his rich butt, somehow.

He invited Brynn and Miles to our mating party, offering free food, flights, and lodging, and both agreed readily.

I COULD TELL he had charmed both of them by the time we were done packing, and I said goodbye while Rafael made a few trips to haul everything to my car.

When I hugged her, Miley whispered, "Let us know if you need us to kill him," but it was half-hearted.

Brynn squeezed me tightly afterward, whispering, "I'm serious about the brothers, Tatum. I want one."

We all laughed, but I could see the honesty in Brynn's eyes. I would have to explain the potential mates thing to her before she got too hopeful.

"Don't forget the next round of seasonal treats," Miley said, as Rafael came back in for the last round of bags.

"I'll get them figured out soon," I agreed, following my demon to the door. "I'm thinking about promoting Sophie to manager and hiring someone else to take her place."

"That's a good idea, if you're going to be busier now." Brynn's gaze flicked to the door, and we all knew she was talking about Rafael.

I had been considering the promotion even before I met Rafe, so I could focus on the desserts as well as have a little more free time. Since he had shaken everything up, it was probably a necessity. I hadn't wanted to take the financial hit, but...

Well, if he was serious about the mating thing, I didn't really need the extra money to go toward a house anymore. My business would still make enough money for me to be independent, and if I wanted a house, I could just pay Rafe back or reluctantly let him pay for it.

It would take me time to decide whether or not I was okay with that, but I couldn't ask my employees to deal with a shitty schedule while I decided.

I'd have to go in and talk to Sophie about it the next day. I already paid her extra to handle the hiring as well as the schedule, so I was sure she would be thrilled about the promotion, and the extra money that came with it.

After one last goodbye, we headed out.

"Did you invite them to go dress shopping with you tomorrow?" Rafael asked, as he drove away. We were still using my car, but he was a good enough driver that I didn't protest when he took the wheel every time. It was kind of nice just to sit instead of having to drive.

"No. Didn't think about it."

"Text them, then. They'll need dresses for the party too; I'll pay for everything."

He told me the name of the store, as well as the time, so I reluctantly sent the message.

ME

Hey. I forgot to tell you, I'm going wedding dress shopping tomorrow. You're invited, if you want to come.

BRYNN

OMG

We'll definitely be there!

MILES

What time, and where?

I relayed the information.

MILES

Please tell me the rich demon is paying.

ME

He is. He says we need four dresses each, and he's paying for you guys too

BRYNN

OMG

MILES

He's trying to seduce us with his money

BRYNN

It's working!

Tell me the brothers will be at the party

"Are your brothers going to the party?" I asked Rafael.

"Yes, Bash and Zander will definitely be there. Our mom would kill them for missing it."

ME

they're going

BRYNN

yessssss

I have four days to seduce one of them.

MILES

Which means I get to try to cock-block you for four days. Yay.

ME

Bad news, B. Rafael said demons rarely have sex with humans.

BRYNN

Really? Why?

MILES

That makes my life much easier

ME

I guess drinking lust from a human takes it away from them, so they're not lusty. To make it fun for the human, the demon would have to resist drinking until they were done, which is difficult.

BRYNN

Now I'm even more intrigued

MILES

Oh great

BRYNN

It will be my mission to seduce one of them into giving it a try.

Rafael parked the car, and I lifted my head.

"This isn't your apartment," I said, frowning as I took in a fancy storefront.

"No, it's not." He stepped out of the car, walking around to open my door. My gaze landed on the sign above the sleek entrance.

Oh.

"I'm not dressed for a ring store, Riffraff," I warned, not bothering to unbuckle my seatbelt. "We can do this another day."

"We can do this now," he corrected.

I scrolled past a few messages between Brynn and Miles, typing a quick message.

ME

Gotta go. Talk later.

Rafael plucked my phone from my hands and tucked it in his pocket.

I huffed at him. "I'm not going into that *very expensive looking* jewelry store without a bra or panties on, Rafael. It's not happening."

His eyes flashed wickedly. "Guess I'll have to pick the ring out myself, then. I'm buying the biggest rock in the store."

With that, he closed the door and strode toward the building.

"Damn you," I hissed, unbuckling fast and throwing the door open again. I caught up to him quickly, and he snagged my hand, grinning as he slipped his fingers between mine. "Maybe I *will* choose the biggest rock in the store, just to spite you."

He laughed. "We both know that's not your style, Tater-tot, but go right ahead."

I flashed him a glare, but he was right. It *wasn't* my style. I wasn't attracted to big and flashy.

Unless we were talking about men, I guess. Because I had proven that I was very much into big and flashy, when that damn demon came into the picture.

WE WALKED around the whole store, trying on rings while sipping complimentary drinks. I ended up picking a silver, artsy-looking bezel-set ring that wouldn't catch on anything. Rafael picked out the diamond to go inside it. His ring would be a simple black band; he wasn't interested in anything else, after we looked around.

I left him to figure out the details when he started talking to the jeweler about letter-graded coloring and different qualities of diamond cuts, wandering over to the necklace and earring section of the store. Something told me it wouldn't do us any good if I had a panic attack about the price.

The woman behind the necklace counter started a conversation with me while I looked.

"How did you and Rafael meet?" she asked, her smile big. She had undoubtedly been told that my mate was about to spend an outrageous amount of money on jewelry, so she needed to be friendly.

I still didn't mind the friendliness, though.

"Oh, he walked into my coffee shop one day, and it went from there." I gave her a quick smile, then lowered my gaze back to the jewelry so she didn't see through me. Nothing I'd said was untrue, so I didn't have a hard time getting it out.

"That's sweet. How long have you been together?"

"Long enough," I said with a laugh, and she laughed too.

Again, not technically a lie.

"What coffee shop do you work at?"

"I own the *Coffee & Toffee* on Jive Street." I gestured in the direction of it.

Her eyes lit up. "Oh my gosh, we all get our drinks from the one on Melody every day! Do you know the owner, Brynn?"

I smiled. "I do. We were roommates up until I moved in with Rafael."

She didn't need to know I was still currently in the process of moving in.

"No way!" She beamed. "That is so cool! Did you open them together?"

I launched into an explanation about how we'd been friends in high school, I went to culinary school afterward, and Brynn and Miles studied marketing and finance respectively. She got a kick out of my story about us meeting for coffee, joking around about how we wished they sold candy too, and how everything grew from there.

When Rafael walked over, wrapping an arm around my waist and pressing a dramatic kiss to my forehead, she had already pulled out her phone and followed all three of our shops on social media.

We headed out soon after, and he didn't release his hold on my waist until we reached the car.

"That wasn't as bad as you thought, huh?" he asked, bumping my hip lightly with his.

"It wasn't," I admitted.

"And I got to hear how you ended up opening your shop, so it worked out for me." He winked at me, and I rolled my eyes.

Of course he had listened in on our conversation. It didn't surprise me in the slightest.

And honestly, I kind of liked that he paid so much attention to me.

He asked me more questions about the coffee shops while he drove, and I had no problem answering. His interest in my business made me feel good, and it was nice to talk to someone other than Brynn and Miles about it.

When we got back to the apartment, we spent a few minutes in his bed together while I fed him—without letting him touch me, again—before I padded back to my own bed, and promptly fell asleep there.

THE NEXT MORNING, I woke up horny, after a night full of steamy dreams. I stumbled to the bathroom, and when I emerged, found Rafael putting my things away in his closet.

Leaning against the wall separating our rooms, I blinked, watching him for a few minutes.

"Bash texted me. Our mom decided she can't wait out the whole week and is getting on a plane tonight, to come and meet you."

Shit.

I rubbed my eyes with the base of my palm. "Great."

"She can't know we're sleeping apart," he explained. "She won't be staying here, obviously, but if she peeks upstairs, she needs to find your things in my closet."

Right.

Cool.

"Okay." I stayed where I was, watching him move.

"The jeweler left me a message; I'll pick up our rings this morning, as well."

I had figured he'd pay extra to get them done fast, so that didn't surprise me. I hoped whatever he paid made staying up all night worth it for the jeweler.

He turned around to put something behind where he had been standing, and I saw a flash of red in his eyes.

He was hungry again.

And on top of that, clearly a little frazzled for some reason. I'd never seen him frazzled before, and I kind of liked it. Not because I wanted him to struggle, but because it made him seem more real, and less perfect.

I didn't want him to feel like crap, though.

So, I slipped down the stairs. I still hadn't taken the time to change, so I was just wearing his shirt and a pair of panties. The underboob sweat was real after those hot dreams, but I wasn't going to bring that up.

Looking through his cabinets quietly, I took stock of his ingredients before making him a quick, sugary cup of coffee that I knew would take the edge off for him. Then, I grabbed a half-empty box of candy from one of our shops and carried both that and the cup back up the stairs.

Rafael inhaled deeply, turning when I reached the closet's entrance. His surprised gaze lingered on the drink, and then lifted to my face. "You made me coffee?"

"Nah, it's for me." I took a tiny sip of the steaming drink.

Definitely not my favorite, but he'd like it.

His lips curved upward as I gave up the act and crossed the large closet, handing him the drink and the chocolates. "Good morning."

"Thanks, Tater-tot."

"No problem, Riffraff." I winked at him, and his lips stretched in a grin before he lifted the mug to his mouth, taking a slow sip.

"Mmm. You're good at that."

"I know." I pretended to fluff my hair, and his chuckle made me smile.

Everything felt *easier* between us.

I decided that was probably because of our conversation the night before, when we'd decided how we were going to handle things.

His declaration that we were at the beginning of a permanent relationship changed my perspective, I supposed.

"Are you going to tell me why you're flustered? I asked, leaning against the wall while he resumed putting my stuff away. The man took frequent breaks to sip coffee and take bites of candy, which made me smile a little.

"I woke up feeling like I was back in prison. I saw the empty room around me when I opened my eyes, and realized I wasn't. When I closed them again, I still felt like I was there, so I got up."

I grimaced. "I can imagine being free again is a hard adjustment."

He made a noise of agreement, and we both grew quiet as he continued.

I didn't expect him to say anything else, but after a few minutes, he spoke again.

"It put things into perspective—being in prison. Starving. Losing control. I had never felt so helpless or hopeless. I clung to the idea of you, to the image of you. I'd never considered that I could die alone, and the thought was terrifying."

"You didn't know what I looked like, did you?"

"I did. Shortly before they locked me up, I followed the pull to your coffee shop and spent a few minutes sitting at a table, watching you. You seemed very at ease, and I admired that."

My throat swelled. "You're way more at ease with yourself than I am."

"A supernatural has to take a mate to experience true contentment. Those of us who stay alone do so because it's easier, not because it's more enjoyable." He took another sip of his drink. "It's nice to be free again, and not to be alone anymore, but it'll take us both time to get used to it."

"We're up for the challenge," I said.

He flashed me a small grin. "Of course we are."

I mirrored his expression, and helped him finish putting everything away.

And when we went to his bed so I could feed him, I even considered letting him touch me. I decided against it, of course —but I considered it.

RAFAEL

WE SPENT the morning at *Coffee & Toffee* while Tatum talked to Sophie about a promotion, then stopped for ingredients for her candy tests on the way back to our apartment. I noticed August, the dragon shifter, tailing us. That was expected. The rules he'd mentioned required him to follow us for six months after my escape, just to make sure I wasn't falling back into my wicked ways.

It was an annoyance, but it gave me an excuse to stay close to Tatum, so I didn't mind.

When we made it home, we spent twenty minutes in my bed while she fed me—still without letting me touch her. Then, I tackled lunch while she got started on her newest attempt at peppermint truffles.

Music played from a speaker she'd brought while we worked separately, and her presence put me at ease in a way little else ever had. She seemed to think everything came simply to me because I was a demon, and didn't understand the depths of an immortal being's struggle with loneliness.

Eternity was a damn long time to be on your own.

Supernaturals kept busy to distract ourselves, and resisted the urge to drag another person into an endless life with us. Mating with someone simply for the sake of having a companion was certainly frowned upon, so it was rare for someone to dare trying it. There was much too high of a risk that the mated pair could despise each other. Even couples who had previously been in love could fall apart in enough time. Love was a choice —and it was one that people got tired of making, at times.

Taking Tatum as my companion the way I had meant I would have to be the certain one. I would hold us together, with grit, willpower, and whatever the hell else I had to.

I made her mine; I would make her enjoy being mine, even if I had to work at it every day for the rest of our lives.

We ate in the kitchen when the food was done, and then shortly afterward, tested her truffles. They were incredible, but she wasn't satisfied, so she made a few notes on her recipe card and made another batch.

When those ones weren't perfect, we cleaned the kitchen together, then picked her friends up. I dropped the three of them off at the dress boutique, then met Zander at a restaurant a few doors down.

We discussed the security he'd put into place for Tatum and her friends for a while, then talked about the four main vampire clans, who we were keeping an eye on. Bash had flown to Dallas to take care of a rogue vampire we'd gotten reports of, which would've been my job before I was tossed in prison.

While the vampire clans were technically supposed to deal with their own rogues, it often took them weeks or months to do so. And in those weeks or months, more unsuspecting humans died and were turned, creating more rogues. It spiraled quickly, and most of the clans didn't care about human lives, so we dealt with it.

A few hours passed before Tatum texted me that they were ready. Zander paid the tab, shooing me out, and I strode back to her car. I intended to replace it with something newer and safer, but I was giving her time to adjust first.

I knew her well enough to know it would take some convincing, too.

The girls were all buzzed and laughing when they climbed into the car. Tatum pulled me down and plopped a kiss on my mouth before I could close her door behind her, then laughed alongside her friends. It was our first kiss, and considering how everything else had gone in our relationship, it seemed quite fitting.

I grinned at her. "How much champagne did you drink?"

"Just a little." She held her thumb and forefinger about an inch apart, and I shook my head at her, closing the door after she tucked her feet safely inside.

"Thanks for the fun, Rafael," Brynn called.

"No problem."

“Can you give my brothers your number?” She giggled. Miley and Tatum snorted, and she laughed, harder. “Can you give your brothers my number, I mean.”

“You’ve got it.” I chuckled to myself, driving back to their place. Miley and Brynn made their way unsteadily to their door, waving at Tatum, and she waved back without hesitation.

Her head leaned up against the window, and I knew the magic in her system would already be weakening the effects of the alcohol. Demons got drunk the same way humans did, but it didn’t last long.

By the time we parked, she seemed almost entirely sober, but still looked calm and relaxed.

She let me help her out, and leaned against me as we walked back to the elevator.

“How was shopping?”

“Fun.” Her smile was genuine, her cheeks still a bit red from the alcohol.

Fuck me, she was the most adorable creature I had ever seen.

“Good.” I couldn’t stop myself from brushing my lips to her forehead, touching her that way.

She stepped a bit closer to me. “Your mom will be here tomorrow?”

“Unfortunately.” I ran my hand slowly over her hip, wishing she was still wearing one of my shirts to give me better access.

“How well do we have to sell it to her?” She leaned in closer, and my arm around her tightened.

"Fairly well. We're sure she has an idea that it's fake, and she wouldn't lie for any of us. She's part of the supernatural government, so she is very particular when it comes to mating. If we can make it seem reasonably real, she won't ask questions or bring up her suspicions."

"Is that supposed to make me feel better?"

"It's just the truth." I brushed my lips to her forehead again.

"We're going to have to practice acting like we're in love, then. She's probably ancient, so she's not an idiot."

I chuckled. "How do you intend to practice that?"

"I have no idea."

The elevator dinged, and we stepped out together. Neither of us made for the stairs, or our beds. I hadn't eaten dinner without her, knowing she'd need food after trying on dresses, and the sun had only just finished setting.

"Sit down. I'll warm up leftovers." I brushed another kiss to her forehead.

Tatum made her way to the couch, sprawling over the cushions and staring out the windows. She seemed to enjoy the view as much as I did, and stared at the mountains intently.

"Pasta or casserole?" I asked her.

"Pasta, always."

I threw our bowls in the microwave one at a time, and then took them to the couch when the food was hot enough.

"We probably shouldn't eat on this expensive couch," Tatum said, as I handed her the bowl.

"What's the point in having a couch if we can't do what we want on it?"

"That's a fair point." She took a bite of her food. Her forehead wrinkled slightly as she considered something.

She took a few more bites before she said, "I think we'll have to practice kissing."

I coughed, nearly choking on the food in my mouth.

That definitely wasn't what I expected her to say.

It was an easy answer, though.

"Alright."

"We should probably share your bed while she's here, too. If she's with your government, we don't want to risk her coming in with coffee or breakfast and finding out that our relationship is fake."

My eyes narrowed.

She quickly clarified, "Not fake—just starting. We don't want her finding out our relationship is just starting. She has the code to get in, doesn't she? Your brothers have the code."

I would give her that one.

"She could guess it, if she doesn't know it already. Bash or Zander likely already gave it to her, though."

She nodded. "We'll practice kissing, and we'll share a bed. That should make us comfortable enough to sell it."

I nodded my agreement and took another bite to stop myself from saying something I might regret.

Like, *"We should practice fucking, too."*

A few minutes passed while we ate, and watched darkness set in over the mountains. The silence was comfortable, and she took my bowl as soon as I finished. My eyes followed her ass to the kitchen. Though I wasn't starving, I could certainly eat if she was the meal.

"Want to watch a movie?"

Her words distracted me, and I lifted my eyes to hers. "Sure."

It had been a long time since I'd seen one.

She rattled off the names of a few that had come out while I was in prison, and I told her to pick one. When she did, I pulled it up and turned it on.

Tatum flipped the lights off on her way to the couch, and when she sat down, she sat close to me. There were only a few inches between our bodies, but the distance was small enough that my attention was fixed on her, not on the TV.

"How close would we sit, if we weren't—" she caught herself before she could say *fake*, and finished, "at the beginning?"

"If we had been together long enough, I'd sit you on my lap."

The faint lust on her skin thickened and grew more vibrant. "We should probably practice that, too."

I made a noise of agreement, grabbing her by her thighs and pulling her close. When her ass and legs were draped over my lap, our bodies perpendicular on the couch, I grabbed a pillow and tucked it beneath her side. She relaxed against it, her lust brighter as she did.

"Thanks."

"Mmhm."

I didn't want to push her, but...

Well, she had started it.

"If we were further into our relationship, I would touch you however I wanted, whenever I wanted," I murmured.

Goosebumps broke out on her skin. "Go ahead."

I ran a hand slowly over her arm, down the curve of her hip, and along her thigh before moving it back up. It slid over her abdomen, afterward, and then up the side of her breast before finding her arm again and repeating the motion.

Her lust grew thicker, and the smell of it became more and more irresistible.

It was her turn to push the boundaries, though, so I didn't ask for more.

Tatum's hips began to move a little, though the way her lips pressed together told me she was trying to stop herself.

I tried to resist—but failed.

Lowering my lips to her ear, I murmured, "If we were further in our bond, I would have made love to you with my fingers, mouth, and cock on every surface in this apartment."

She shuddered.

I continued touching her lightly, lifting my head and waiting for her to set the pace.

To offer me more.

There was a chance she wouldn't do it—but there was also a damn good chance she would.

The movie still played, but neither of us paid it any attention.

Tatum finally pushed my hand off her body and sat up, turning so she could straddle me. Her knees went on either side of my hips, and her hands landed on my chest.

I couldn't have told you what the movie was about. Or what genre it was. Or hell, anything else.

But Tatum's core was pressed to my erection, and damn, I wanted her more than I'd ever wanted anything.

"We just need to practice," she whispered.

I nodded, not trusting myself to speak.

She leaned in closer, her eyes on my lips. "It's been a long time since I kissed anyone. I—"

I couldn't wait any longer, and captured her mouth with my own. I didn't waste time with a chaste, sweet kiss; I slipped my tongue into her mouth and dragged it along hers.

She tightened her grip on my shirt and leaned in closer as her tongue moved with mine. My hands found her ass and lifted her higher, rolling her clit against my cock in a way that made us both groan.

Her hips rocked, dragging me closer to the edge of pleasure with every motion.

I wanted her.

I needed her.

Nothing else would be enough.

I would wait as long as she asked me to—but damn it would be torture.

We kissed and moved together until she was groaning, her lust so thick in the air I could've fed from it without trying.

She hadn't finished—she was too well-pleasured to lose control like that on my cock, with clothes separating us.

"I'm so close," she moaned into my mouth, pulling away long enough to push her hair from her face. Her chest rose and fell rapidly, and her light green eyes were bright with desire.

"Do you trust me?"

She laughed breathlessly. "No, Riffraff."

I chuckled, grabbing the hem of her shirt. "Do you trust me to take care of you?"

Her grin faded, but the light in her eyes didn't budge. "Maybe I do."

I tugged her shirt over her head, revealing a black lace bra. It was molded to the sexy curve of her breasts, and shit, I wanted to take her nipples in my mouth.

Reaching around her back, I slowly unbuckled the bra.

"What are you doing?" Her expression grew a little uncertain.

"Trust me," I repeated.

Her bra fell away, revealing a set of perfect breasts, and her breath hitched.

"You're going to ride my cock," I told her matter-of-factly, then maneuvered her pants down her thighs and to the ground.

"Wait," she protested, catching my hands. "I—"

"Through my shorts, Tater-tot." I flashed her a grin, and her protest vanished. Her panties joined the rest of her clothes on

the floor, and I spread her thighs open, taking in every inch of her slick, needy core. "Damn, you're gorgeous."

Her face flushed, and the redness spread over her neck and down her chest.

I loved that I could make her blush like that.

My shirt went over my head. After unbuttoning my jeans, I stood long enough to step out of them too. Tatum's eyes were wide as they took me in like I had her; the boxer-briefs I wore barely hid a thing.

"You're huge."

"I know." I sat back down, and she laughed when I grinned at her again.

"You're too cocky for your own good," she said, but when I grabbed her by the thighs, she didn't make a sound of protest.

My cock throbbed when I set her back on my lap. When I looked down and saw her bare breasts nearly touching my chest, it throbbed again.

"You didn't feed yet?" She slid her hands over my chest, moving her fingers on my pecs before sliding them down my abdomen.

"No. This isn't about my hunger." I slowly dragged my hands up the backs of her thighs, and her hips arched. She sucked in a breath when I gripped thick handfuls of her ass, and she rocked against me. Her bare breasts pressed against my chest, and I gritted my teeth against the need to find my release.

"What's it about, then?"

"Practice." I recaptured her mouth, and she moaned. Her hips began to rock faster, the motions growing less controlled as she neared the edge.

Her body arched violently, and she cried out into my mouth as she found her climax on my cock.

"Shit, that was better than the vibrator," she groaned, her bare breasts still against me.

My cock throbbed hard.

I set her on the couch, brushing my lips to her mouth for a heartbeat before I strode to the bathroom.

The door closed behind me, and stripped my shorts off, taking my cock in hand.

I was too damn close not to.

She turned the doorknob mid-stroke, and my gaze met hers as she took me in, bare-assed and jerking off.

I slid my hand around the head of my cock, balls tightening with her attention.

"Keep going," she said, her words breathy.

"Get in here so I can look at you," I growled back.

She stepped in and closed the door behind her.

My body nearly vibrated with the ferocity of my need.

She took another step in, and took my cock in her hand.

My face twisted as I fought not to lose control.

"You're even bigger than I thought," she admitted, slowly dragging her hand down my length.

It was too much.

I snarled, gripping her hand on my cock as I covered her bare stomach with my release.

The pleasure was overwhelming, and the satisfaction was immediate.

When I got myself off, it hardly took off the edge of the [illegible]. She was what I needed [illegible] the only thing that could bring me relief.

[illegible]

[illegible]

[illegible]

It was too much.

I snarled, gripping her hand on my cock as I covered her bare stomach with my release.

The pleasure was overwhelming, and the satisfaction was immediate.

When I got myself off, it barely took off the edge of the need. She was what I needed—she was the only thing that could bring me relief.

I crushed her to my chest, neither of us paying any mind to the slickness between us.

She hugged me back, her arms almost as tight around me as mine were around her. "I don't think we need any practice."

A rough chuckle rolled through me. "I think we need all the practice there is."

But when she pulled away, I simply cleaned her up before following her back to the couch. She pulled my t-shirt on and I stepped into my joggers, but the rest of our clothes remained strewn on the ground as we started the movie over.

Neither of us brought up practice again when she draped her legs and ass over my lap.

eleven

TATUM

RAFAEL DRANK my lust little by little throughout the movie, never taking enough to shift, but still filling himself up. His hands moved slowly over my legs, and I wasn't sure whether he was touching me for the sake of my lust, or just because he wanted to.

Something told me it was the second option, so I ignored that something.

The touch on my thighs grew less sexy and more comfortable as I got used to it, and I found myself dozing off. At some point, I fell asleep entirely.

I WOKE up when the couch disappeared from beneath me, and found myself in Rafael's arms. "I'm taking you to my bed. My mom's plane lands early," he murmured.

I nodded and curled up closer to his bare chest.

The man was ridiculously warm.

I needed to remind myself that he was a criminal, but...

He was only killing vampires.

And only vampires who had already killed humans.

I could convince myself to believe a lot of things, but I didn't think I could convince myself to believe that one any longer.

The man wasn't a criminal.

He had been put in jail for protecting humans.

I was way too tired to consider the injustice of that.

When he tucked us both into his bed, I rolled closer to him. He pulled me against his side, and I loved the way his skin felt against mine.

I was insane for sleeping with him so fast.

I had to be insane for it.

But I didn't have the heart to care. Not when he felt so good, and made me feel so good.

I fell asleep in his arms, more content than I had been in years.

IN THE MORNING, I woke up from sexy, sexy dreams to hushed voices in the kitchen again. Really, Rafael's apartment was the worst design for someone trying to sleep while anyone else was home.

I rolled over—and then fell off the bed with a yelp, followed by a crash.

A groaned laugh escaped me.

Yeah, I'd just fallen out of his bed.

Great.

"Tater-tot?" Rafael's voice floated up to me from the kitchen. "What happened?"

"I'm fine," I called back, sitting up and pushing my hair off my face.

His footsteps were on the stairs a minute later, and he entered the room in the same moment I stood up.

Yep, stood up too quickly and stumbled. That time, I caught myself on the bed, at least.

His lips curved at the sight of me. "You don't look broken, thankfully."

"Luckily for you, I'm not."

I crossed the room, taking him in. He'd put on a sleek sports coat, a button-down shirt, and some nice pants and shoes. He'd also had his hair cut like Sebastian's, but a little longer and less perfect.

In short, he *looked* rich for the first time since we'd met.

Rich and I... we had a past.

And we didn't get along.

I was used to seeing him casual and messy, with joggers and a tee, so I was not at all prepared for the weird feelings that rolled through me at the sight of him. "What happened to your hair, and what the hell are you wearing?"

"I got a much-needed haircut, and I think these are clothes." He glanced down at himself. "Yep. Just clothes."

My lips pressed together.

He pulled me into his arms without questioning my problem with his haircut and clothing, and murmured, "I think these lips need to look kissed."

Did I protest?

No, I did not.

My weird feelings also didn't vanish, though.

He kissed me slowly and passionately, and I kissed him back with the same fire, rising up on my tiptoes as he tilted my head to deepen the kiss.

After a few minutes, I pulled my mouth away from his and asked quietly, "Your mom's here?"

"Both of my parents, and my brothers," he confirmed. "We're going to breakfast. The reservation's in forty minutes."

Shit.

I pushed hair out of my face again with a shaky hand. "Next time, wake me up before they get here so I can get my crap together."

"Will do." He kissed me again, briefly, and then sucked lightly on my neck. My eyes fluttered closed, and I tried not to let him affect me as much as we both knew he would.

"Your parents' names are..."

"Anastasia and Eldrich." He released my throat, reluctantly leaving it alone.

I repeated their names in my mind a few times, and then realized Rafael hadn't gone anywhere. "You don't need to wait for me. I have no problem finding something else to do while you guys go to breakfast."

His eyes narrowed. "You and I are a packaged deal now, Tater-tot. I'm going, so you're going."

I grimaced.

There was no real way to argue against that.

I didn't have anything I thought would look decent next to Rafael's damn *sports coat*, so I told him to find me something to wear while I did my makeup. The only clothing I had for special occasions was a mini skirt and matching top that Brynn had talked me into buying a few years earlier, which obviously wouldn't work for brunch.

The mascara and eyeliner went on in the fanciest way I knew—which wasn't at all fancy—and then I tied my hair up in a bun and called it good.

Rafael was leaned up against the bathroom door with my clothes when I finished, so I plucked them from his hands.

The jeans and simple top would make me look ridiculous when I walked next to him, but even if I had an elegant skirt or dress, I wouldn't have wanted to wear it. So, I needed to figure out how to embrace my casual self.

The other option was changing my wardrobe for a man, and I had absolutely no intention of doing that.

After getting dressed in the bathroom, I reluctantly let him tow me down the stairs. My socked feet padded against the tile, and my hand clutched Rafael's.

Four sets of eyes were on us as we hit the bottom of the stairs.

His mother, Anastasia, was just as gorgeous as I expected. She had tan skin, straight, shiny black hair that fell to the middle of her back, and a killer body showcased by the tasteful black wrap dress she wore. Her eyes were bright, and her lips formed a half-smile that told me absolutely nothing about what she was truly thinking or feeling.

His dad, Eldrich, looked a lot like him and his brothers, but his skin was a few shades darker than theirs, and his hair was curly while theirs only had waves. His position was relaxed as he leaned against the wall nearest to the door. Though his gaze was curious, it wasn't judgmental or accusatory.

"Mom, dad, this is Tatum. Tatum, meet my parents." Rafael gestured toward them, and I forced my friendliest coffee-shop-smile to my face.

"Hi," I said, feeling even more awkward as I did.

Rafael tucked me closer to his side, and I leaned against him a bit more in hopes it would ease the awkwardness.

And maybe, sell the charade a little better.

Anastasia's smile widened.

I still wasn't sure if it was genuine.

"Welcome to the family, Tatum. I've been waiting a damn long time for one of my boys to finally put an end to their eternal bachelor-hoods."

Zander snorted.

Sebastian grimaced.

Amusement colored Eldrich's gaze.

Rafael laughed, loudly. "Finally, the pestering ends."

"For you, at least." She winked at me and then turned her gaze to her other two sons. "Bash, you have a potential mate in this city too, right?"

"He shouldn't have told you that," Zander said.

"Perhaps Tatum will succeed at hunting her down, unlike me," she tossed back.

Maybe her smile was genuine, after all.

"You've tried to hunt their potential mates down?" I asked.

"Dozens of times, in a handful of cities. Potential mates are notoriously difficult to walk away from, after you've met them. Which is why they don't tell anyone, including each other, where their mates are located."

"So yes, our mother has been trying to entrap us for decades," Zander drawled.

"If making your life better and your hunger easier to manage is considered entrapment these days, then yes, I have been trying to entrap you." She brushed the front of her dress off, though I didn't see any dust, crumbs, or lint anywhere. "We need to get going. Ready?"

Everyone agreed, and shuffled toward the door. I stepped into my boots before Rafael could lead me outside. The keys in his hand definitely weren't mine—and something told me I was finally going to see his car.

The elevator carried us down quickly. In the parking garage, Anastasia and Eldrich followed Zander and Sebastian rather than sticking with us.

"We'll see you there," Anastasia called over her shoulder.

"Good work, Tater-tot." He kissed my cheek as we crossed the garage, and I pushed his face away from mine, which made him chuckle.

I noticed the dragon shifter from my coffee shop sitting in a car near the elevator's opening, and nearly stumbled. When Rafael lifted a hand to him in greeting, I did the same.

"You're finally going to show me your car, huh?" I asked him, as we approached a row of luxury vehicles. My gaze scanned all of them, trying to determine which one was Rafael's, but I couldn't decide.

All of them were ridiculously priced, and nowhere near reasonable or necessary.

"Finally," he grinned, leading me to the far end of the row, behind the vehicles I had seen.

And right up to a shiny, silver car that was identical to my own, but a dozen years newer.

I stopped in my tracks.

Rafael's grin widened. "Quite the expensive car, wouldn't you say?"

I blinked.

I was confident it had been pimped out with all the fanciest options the manufacturer offered, and probably a few extras as well, but...

It was *my* car.

Or similar enough to my car that I couldn't judge him for it.

"You have good taste in vehicles," I finally said, slightly reluctant. "Unless you bought this after we met, just so I couldn't judge you."

He laughed. "I bought it when I moved here before I went to prison. A have an older version in red at my house back in Wolfcrest, too."

We buckled up, and I couldn't help but admire the vehicle as he pulled out of the garage. It was gorgeous. Really, really gorgeous.

And knowing that he could've bought anything he wanted, but went with a reasonable vehicle, made me respect him just a little more.

EATING breakfast with his family was surprisingly nice. I already knew his brothers were friendly, and they included me in the conversations like I already belonged. Rafael kept touching my hand and leg, and putting his arm over my shoulders, which I liked. It sold the picture we were putting on, but honestly, it didn't feel like a lie.

It just felt like we were at our beginning, the way he had said.

Anastasia sat on my other side throughout the meal, which surprised me, but I wasn't uncomfortable with it. I showed her pictures of my party dresses before we ate, and she oohed and ahhed over them with me. It felt easier to call them party dresses than wedding dresses, and only one of them was white, so it seemed fitting.

She didn't judge me for it, either.

As the meal came to an end, she entertained all of us with stories about the weeks she'd spent with her sons over the years. She'd refuse to leave their sides in hopes that they'd spill the beans about where their potential mates were located—either accidentally, or because they got tired of her pestering. It had yet to work, but she hadn't given up hope yet.

"How would you know if someone was their potential mate, if they didn't tell you?" I asked, curiosity taking ahold of me.

She flashed me a smile. "It's impossible for a demon to truly ignore his or her fated mate, Tatum. If she speaks, he listens. If he moves, her eyes follow him. When you know what you're looking for, it's easy enough to spot."

"And she's really, *really* nosy," Eldrich added, his arm going around her waist.

She laughed loudly, and leaned a little closer to him. "You're not wrong, honey."

They were adorable together.

He was the quiet one, she was the loud one, and from what I had seen, they just *worked.*

After the meal, everyone went back to Rafael's apartment. The guys sat on the couch, chatting about vampires. I had to make a few batches of different types of candies for the shop, so I chatted with Anastasia while I baked. She tied an apron around her waist and joined me, and we talked while we worked.

Despite what I would've expected, it was actually a lot of fun.

And when I watched her feed Eldrich one of my truffles, I couldn't hide my smile.

They were too damn sweet.

• • •

IT WAS late in the evening when everyone finally cleared out. Rafael's eyes weren't glowing, but I noticed the color in them was muddled when he sat on one of the stools after locking the door behind his family.

I hadn't stepped away to feed him at all that day, and he hadn't asked me to, so it didn't really cross my mind. The dynamic between us felt a little weirder with his haircut and change of clothing.

I finished boxing up the last of my treats to take to the shops—thankfully, they lasted longer than baked goods or hot meals, so I had more freedom with the frequency I had to make them—and then leaned over the counter on my forearms. My hair fell onto the countertop with me, and my face was only a few feet from Rafael's when it did.

"You are really damn good with my family," he told me simply, moving in closer too. His hand lifted to cradle my cheek, and I closed my eyes for a moment, enjoying the soft touch.

"They're not difficult to be good with. I like them."

"They like you too." He leaned in further and brushed his lips to mine. The kiss was slow and soft, until he pulled away.

A moment later, he took me into his arms and kissed me again.

The second kiss was like the first, but better.

So much better.

Still slow, and still soft, but so damn much more intimate. His hands found my hips and he turned me until my ass was pressed against the cabinets while we kissed.

Without pulling away, he lifted me onto the counter.

"Tell me I can touch you," he murmured against my lips.

"You can touch me," I said, before he stole my mouth again.

His hands worked my jeans and panties down to my knees as he continued kissing me, and we both groaned when his fingers slipped between my thighs and worked my clit.

The kiss ended, but my fingers dug into the thick, ropy muscles of his arms as I struggled to catch my breath. He brought me to orgasm quickly—so damn quickly—drinking in my lust as he did.

It wasn't enough.

It was never enough for him.

He continued playing with my clit until I'd lost control again, and his lust was finally sated.

Then, he pulled my pants and panties back into place and carried both me and my treats back out to his car. His hand remained planted on my thigh while he drove us to all three shops, only releasing me long enough to let me run my boxes in so they'd be ready to sell in the morning.

When we got in bed together that night, we ended up making out until we'd both lost control—me, on his fingers, and him, all over my abdomen.

The lines between us were beginning to blur... and I wasn't sure how to fight it.

Even more than that, I wasn't sure if I *wanted* to fight it.

And that made everything so much more confusing.

twelve

TATUM

THE NEXT FEW days passed similarly, with a few more sightings of the dragon shifter who had been sent to keep an eye on us. His name was August, Rafael said, and he was going to be stuck in town watching us for about six months.

We spent all of our time with his family, which was ridiculously comfortable.

His parents flew back home three days later, which left us alone again.

Rafael and I quickly fell into a rhythm.

I fed him in the morning and evening, and we both brought each other pleasure every time. We didn't bring mouths or demon forms into it, or have full-on sex, but we wanted to.

Both of us were just waiting for the other person to take us to the next level, and neither of us did.

When we got out of his bed, I spent the morning working on food for the coffee shop or trying to perfect my newest recipes, and he either helped or worked on his laptop.

I took care of lunch for us, either by cooking or heating up left-overs. When we were done eating, we stopped in at my coffee shop once every few days, to make sure things were going well. The holiday season was in full-swing, so it was hectic.

We usually saw August when we went there. I gave him complimentary coffee every day to make up for lying to him, even though he was a grumpy bastard.

In the late afternoons, I worked more, then went to yoga and self-defense on the respective nights Miley and Brynn had convinced me to sign up for. When I was done—or earlier, if there were no classes—Rafael and I watched movies, eating the food he either cooked or bought for us for dinner.

Neither of us suggested I should move back to my own bed.

We both enjoyed our *arrangement* too much for that.

Life was peaceful, and I was enjoying being mated more than I ever would've imagined.

Rafael kept a steady supply of red roses in the kitchen, the bathrooms, and our bedroom, and they always had funny little handwritten notes attached to them.

> *I love checking out your ass every time you bend over to go through the cabinets.*

> *It's sexy how your voice changes when you're annoyed that your recipes aren't perfect.*

I love the way your nose twitches when you focus.

The freckle inside your thigh wants you to let me lick it.

It's hot how happy you get when you bite into something you love.

I love the way your face twists when you climax.

Even though I wanted to complain about them at first, I loved them.

I really, really did.

It was nice having something beautiful to look at, but it was nicer to see his thoughts about me on paper. I caught him writing the notes on a few occasions, so I didn't have any question about whether or not it was him.

He didn't tell me anything else about him and his brothers' work, but when I asked about them, he said there was a vampire clan forming in Scale Ridge for the first time ever. Zander and Sebastian were dealing with it, and I knew Rafael wanted to help, even though he was being stalked by a dragon shifter and clearly couldn't risk leaving.

THE WEEKS PASSED QUICKLY. Thanksgiving came and went, with Miley joining me, Rafael, and his family for a homemade dinner. Before I knew it, two months had gone by. He was still wearing sports coats and expensive pants every day too, and it still weirded me out. I had always said I wouldn't marry a rich man, and there I was... more than married to a rich man.

And enjoying it, too.

I still wished he'd let his hair grow out a bit and start wearing joggers again, but I didn't say that aloud. I wouldn't have changed my clothes for him, so I wouldn't ask him to change his for me. I was getting used to the suits, slowly.

It wasn't like they made him less attractive. It was just a different vibe.

The time came to fly out to our mating celebration, so I left Sophie and the other two shops with enough candy to get through two weeks, even though we were only going to be gone for five days. We packed quickly after that, and headed to the airport.

Rafael had bought first-class tickets for both of us and my best friends (apparently private jets were bad for the environment, on top of being a waste of money), so even though the party was halfway across the country, we'd survive it just fine.

Brynn was practically bursting with excitement, and Miles was trying to act like she wasn't thrilled.

The flight went by quickly.

The drive to the beachfront resort wasn't bad, either.

And soon enough, all of us were making our way to our rooms after checking in. Their rooms were down the hall from ours, and across from each other, so I hoped it would be fun for them.

WE HAD a few hours to kill before the party started that night with a masquerade ball of all things, so we all dropped our stuff in our ridiculously large rooms before changing and heading out to the beach.

"I'd rather fuck you in this bikini than let you out to socialize with people we both know," Rafael murmured into my ear as the elevator lowered.

I laughed, and when I pushed him away half-heartedly, he just grinned and pulled me closer. My simple white bikini was nothing fancy, but I liked it.

My family beat us there by a few hours, and had already claimed a few chairs out on the sand. My stomach clenched at the knowledge that I was about to introduce them to my mate, but Rafael wrapped an arm around my waist, squeezing lightly to comfort me.

It only helped a little, but a little was better than nothing.

We reached the beach far too quickly, and I immediately saw my mom off to our left, standing up and waving at us.

"Good luck with your family!" Brynn said cheerfully, before grabbing Miley's arm and trying to tow her to our right.

"Do you want us to help with your family?" Miles asked, digging her heels into the sand to buy time. "I can toe-off with your brother, if you need me to."

I tried to force a smile, but it came out a grimace. "I'll be fine. Thanks, though. Have fun."

She nodded, flashed Rafael a look of warning, and then let Brynn pull her down the beach.

"What's the story with your brother?" Rafael asked me, squeezing my hip lightly.

"One you don't need to worry about." I brushed hair out of my eyes. "Let's get this over with."

He looked like he wanted to argue, but he resisted the urge as we made our way toward my family. I waved back at my mom, so she knew we saw her.

Though she stopped waving, she remained standing, with her arms folded across her chest.

She had on a modest one-piece swimsuit that fit her well, hiding the scars from the last handful of surgeries she'd had done. Despite the distance between us, I could tell her chest was much bigger than the last time I'd seen her—and I knew her well enough to know that if she'd had her boobs done, she'd had her butt done too.

"Her name is Linda, your dad is Doug, and your brother is Max?"

"And his wife is Alena," I agreed. "Their dog is Lily. They carry her around like a purse but talk about her like she's a child, so prepare yourself."

He snorted. "Lovely."

I probably should've warned him about my family's dynamics, but wasn't sure how. So, I stayed quiet.

"Tatum!" my mom exclaimed, putting an arm around me for a half-hug and then air-kissing my cheeks. "And this is the man who stole my daughter's heart in secret. It's Rafael Vill*ane*, correct?"

She smiled up at him brightly, knowing damn well she had his name wrong. No one could play the weaponized incompetence card like my mother.

"Vill*in*, actually, though I would prefer it pronounced your way." He winked at her, and I swear, the woman nearly swooned. "And you're Linda Bennett, I'd gather. A woman as beautiful as her name."

She laughed airily. "Oh, you're a charmer."

He was, and he knew it.

"You have to introduce me to your mother when she arrives. Anastasia really picked the most beautiful resort. We usually stay at the Herron when we come here—but now, we know better."

There she went, name-dropping a ritzy resort that Rafael most definitely would've heard of.

Rafael smiled, and my mom fanned her face. "Alena! Come over and meet Rafael."

It didn't pass my notice that she didn't introduce him as *Tatum's fiancé, Tatum's mate*, or even *Tatum's sweetheart*. His status was far above mine to my family. They would try like hell to schmooze him, in an attempt to slide into his social circle.

Hence the reason I hadn't seen them in a long time, and had no desire to do so.

My sister-in-law hurried over, her massive chest bouncing with the motion. She was wearing what had to be the world's tiniest black bikini, so pretty much every inch of her was exposed. And of course, her tiny, fluffy dog was tucked under her arm, squished up against her side. One of her boobs bumped poor Lily in the face, and I felt bad for the spoiled little creature.

It wasn't the surgeries or the enhanced body parts I had a problem with—it was the fake personalities that went along with them.

And the schmoozing.

And the obsession with bank accounts and social statuses.

I saw the shock in Alena's eyes when she saw the man at my side, and it registered in her mind that *this* was Rafael. My brother had money, but he was a dick. He was moderately attractive, but no one could compare to the level of gorgeous my demon basically radiated.

"Hello, Rafael." She smiled her biggest, most seductive smile and put her shoulders back a bit, slyly making her boobs look bigger.

Newsflash—they didn't need any help in that department.

Though I didn't envy my mother or Elena, or even *like* them, I couldn't help but feel a bit self-conscious looking at them. I wasn't even sure if I'd remembered to put mascara and eyeliner on that day. And I liked the way I looked, but I knew I didn't look anywhere near as perfect as they did.

Alena offered him a hand, and I was sure she expected him to kiss it.

"Nice to meet you. That's Lily, I take it," Rafael said, ignoring her hand with another charming smile. He didn't so much as look down at the dog, just gesturing to it.

My own lips curved in the beginning of a smile.

He had to know he would've gotten an eyeful of boob if he looked down, and he hadn't done so. If I had to put money on his reasoning, I would've bet that he did so out of respect for me.

Alena's eyes lit up. "Isn't she the cutest? We love her to death." She lifted the tiny dog up higher, and Rafael scratched the furball behind the ears.

"The cutest," he agreed, clearly still laying on the charm. And it still seemed to be working, unsurprisingly.

The man was the full package—pun intended.

"So this is the demon who stole my daughter," my dad said, finally setting his phone down on his chair and joining the conversation. His arm went over my mom's shoulder, and she flashed him an annoyed expression that vanished before she looked back at us.

Rafael chuckled like the joke was actually funny. "I'd say yes, but it's safe to say Tatum is the one who stole me." He shook my dad's hand.

"Welcome to the family, son."

The words were similar to the ones Anastasia had said to me, but with none of the emotion behind them.

And of course, my dad tagged on, "We need to get together and talk business soon."

"I don't mix business and family, but I appreciate the sentiment." He was still smiling, and thick, heavy appreciation welled in my chest.

I could *not* handle any more time with my family in my life, even if it was about business. After the party was over, I would most definitely return to coming up with excuses for why I couldn't attend the vacations that were thinly-veiled attempts to convince me to start living the way my family wanted me to live.

"We'll have to talk about that, too." My dad grinned, but there was no humor behind it. Only the sharp hunger of a man who had realized he was outmatched, and decided he was going to fight his way to equality.

Considering Rafael's family had been around for an undefined amount of time, I didn't think he had a shot.

Rafael grinned back, though there was no humor in his expression either. He was acting charming, but there was none of his usual warmth in anything he'd said since he started interacting with my family.

"Come meet your sister's fiancé, Maximus," my dad commanded. A few heads nearby turned at the volume of his voice.

I wanted to cover my face and hide, but obviously, that wasn't an option.

Max finally set his own phone down and stepped up to the group. "Seems like Tatum has finally brought some money to the table," he drawled, offering Rafael a hand.

Rafe's eyes narrowed, ignoring Max's outstretched hand. "Excuse me?"

Once again, I wanted to cover my face.

"Oh, he's just joking. Max is the funny one in the family," Alena said, giving an over-the-top laugh. She put her hand to his bare chest, and nudged his outstretched hand down.

My mom laughed with her, and I fought the urge to cringe at the discomfort.

And, well, the insult.

"I don't see how that was a joke," Rafael said, his voice calm and his gaze relaxed once again. He tucked me tighter to his side, bending down to brush a kiss to my forehead.

My brother's face reddened. "She went to *culinary school.*"

"So did my mother. Are you suggesting that people who can cook don't deserve the same amount of respect as those who can run a business?"

His face reddened further.

"Of course that's not what he meant," my father put in. "But we raised our children with plans to succeed greatly, in a lot more than cooking. If she'd agreed to put her hand in the family business, she—"

Rafael's voice was still calm as he said, "Tatum has been incredibly successful with her *own* business, managing to make more than enough money while also creating unique recipes that may as well be art. If you don't respect my mate, it would be wise to leave now. You'll find that demons have little tolerance for those who mistreat their own blood relatives."

My dad blinked.

No one *ever* talked to him like that.

Max's face was still getting redder.

Honestly, I was so damn stunned by how the conversation had turned, I didn't even know what to think or say.

"Oh, they were both just joking," my mom said quickly, forcing another laugh. Alena joined her, but this time, Rafael didn't smile.

"Excuse us, we have guests to greet," he said instead. "It was truly a pleasure meeting you."

I could hear the sarcasm in his voice, but it was subtle enough that I doubted my family would catch it.

"Holy shit," I whispered to him, as we strode away together.

"You could've warned me we were walking into a snake pit," he murmured back.

"Sorry."

He squeezed my hip lightly, where his hand was still resting. "Don't apologize. We'll talk about why later. How much of a dick was Max growing up?"

My throat swelled.

If Rafael hadn't just raked him and my dad through the coals, I wouldn't have been comfortable opening up. But he had, so I was. "He bullied me constantly. There's only a year and a half between us, so... yeah. It was bad. They always took his side."

"And culinary school tipped it over the edge?"

I made a noise of agreement. "They told me they were transferring my trust fund into his account if I applied. I transferred it myself, and moved out a few hours later. If my grandma had still been alive, she would've supported me, but she had been gone for a few years by then."

"Damn."

I nodded.

He squeezed my hip again. "Well, I'm glad you got out when you did. I prefer you as you are."

"You'd like the fake boobs, if I had them," I countered.

He laughed—a booming laugh that made people turn their heads again. This time, a few of them grinned back when they did. "Why would I want to change perfection?"

"I still think you're lying," I warned, though I couldn't hide my smile.

"I'll have to remind you how perfect I find them when we're alone tonight, then."

My smile widened, and he led me over to a tent. "Ready to meet some more demons, Tater-tot?"

"*So* ready, Riffraff."

He laughed again at my nickname for him, pulling me even closer as we approached another umbrella.

thirteen

TATUM

WE SPENT a few hours on the beach as he introduced me around. I wouldn't remember the names of the people he introduced me to, but most of them seemed nice enough that I didn't think they'd be offended.

Rafael and I went back to our room to grab my dresses, then walked down the hall with all four of the heavy, luxurious bags. He held them up off the ground so they didn't drag, and I glanced up at him. "So, how weird is this thing going to be?"

He grinned. "Pretty weird. But as long as no one kisses you, I won't have to kill anyone."

I snorted. "That makes me feel better."

"You'll have fun. The whole purpose is to remind me how lucky I am that you're mine, so it'll be better for you than for me. You're the one being celebrated, and you deserve it." The words were simple, but they made me happy.

Really, really happy.

“Thanks, I think.”

He chuckled, lifting my knuckles to his lips and brushing a kiss to them.

“Thanks for not flirting with Alena, too,” I added, my voice a bit softer. I didn’t want to admit it, but that would’ve killed me a little bit. And not in a good way.

“I have no interest in your sister-in-law, or anyone else for that matter. You’re it for me, remember?” he set my hand on the center of his chest, so I could feel his heart beating steadily against my palm.

“I remember.”

He knocked on Brynn’s door, and she threw it open a minute later, beaming. She and Miles had headed back a few minutes before us, since we were caught up in a conversation with someone Rafael had worked with at some point.

“Hey, come in!” she waved me into her room, which was just as oversized as ours. “Hang those up, and then get out of here,” she commanded Rafael.

He did as instructed, giving me a quick kiss before he strode out of the room.

Miley slipped inside, and it clicked shut behind her. “He knows he doesn’t have to pretend in front of us, right?”

My face warmed.

Brynn smiled. “I don’t think he’s pretending, Miles. When a supernatural being takes a mate, it’s forever. Regardless of how it comes about.”

Both of us turned our attention to our blonde, happy friend. "How do you know that?" Miley asked, suspicious.

Her cheeks pinked. "It's just something I've heard."

Miley's eyes narrowed at her. "No way is that the full story. Spill it, B."

Her face grew pinker. "I can't. I'd tell you if I could, but I really can't."

"Are you secretly mated to someone?" I asked.

"No, no, nothing like that. It's a family thing."

"You're secretly a supernatural?" Miley demanded, her voice louder than usual.

"No, I'm not! I'm just related to them. Do these hips really look like supernatural hips?" She turned her hips. The woman had gorgeous curves, but she was thicker than any supernatural I'd seen. Most of their genes kept them effortlessly in shape.

Which... were my genes, now.

Yikes.

It was weird to think of myself as a supernatural. I'd fed on Rafael a few times, while he was feeding on me, but that was the extent of my magic. That, and my clear skin.

"I don't know enough about supernaturals to say," Miley said, her eyes still a bit narrowed.

"Well believe me, they're not. Most of them are naturally super athletic. Even turned supernaturals don't usually have curves, though I'm not sure how it would work for turned demons..." she eyed my body critically.

“I didn’t shrink when I became a demon,” I pointed out. “And I’m not curvy, but I’m definitely not skinny.”

“Hmm. We’ll have to check out the mated pairs while we’re at the ball tonight to see if we can figure it out,” Brynn decided. “Or I can just ask my new mother-in-law.”

Miley grimaced.

Brynn’s eyes lit up. “I forgot about that. Do it!”

I texted her quickly.

ME

Hey! This is really random, but do turned demons get skinnier or stronger?

ANASTASIA

I only know one male demon who mated with a human woman, and her size didn’t change. Historically, most of us only pair up with each other <3

I relayed the information, and Brynn frowned. “Damn. Guess I’ll have to lay off the chocolates if I want to make my ass shrink.”

“Girl, your ass is perfect the way it is. Eat the chocolate.” Miley smacked her butt lightly, making her laugh and me grin.

We migrated to the bathroom, chatting as we took turns showering off the sand, then started doing our hair and makeup. Brynn had declared that I didn’t need makeup thanks to my new *demonic glow* (which was a compliment, though it felt like an insult), but I made Miley put eyeliner on me since she was better with it than I was, and then I swiped a little mascara on.

"So the goal tonight is to hook up with someone, right?" Brynn checked.

I lifted my hands. "I don't care what you do, as long as you're there for the wedding tomorrow just before lunch." They were the only bridesmaids, and I didn't want to look like a moron if they didn't show up.

Plus Rafael's brothers would be there as the groomsmen, so the numbers wouldn't be balanced if they were gone.

"We'll be there," Miley said firmly. "Even if Brynn talks someone into taking her back to their room."

She grinned. "I'll find someone to take *you* back to their room, too."

"Please, we all know Miles will only go for it if she can bring him back to *her* room, so she can make *him* do the walk of shame," I tossed back with a grin.

Both of them laughed—though Miley's laugh was a little sheepish. "You're not wrong."

"It'll be fun, you'll see." Brynn nudged her on the arm. "Maybe we can both snag a demon. I've got my fingers crossed that one of those gorgeous bastards will realize I'm his potential mate tonight."

It was highly unlikely, but I smiled anyway. "I'll cross my fingers for you."

"I won't. I'm still annoyed that you're keeping supernatural secrets from us," Miley grumbled.

"Believe me, I would tell you if I could." She gave Miley a quick hug. Though Miles looked disgruntled, her expression relaxed a little, and we continued getting ready.

• • •

WITH MY MASSIVE, heavy skirt flowing around me in a huge puff of fabric, I took a few steps back. I was trying to see myself in the mirror to get a whole picture of my dress, but it wasn't working.

The damn thing was too big.

Still, I loved it. I had never considered myself someone who would want a princess dress, but I'd wanted a princess dress.

For one of the nights, at least.

Luckily, the room was big enough that I finally made it back far enough to see the whole picture of myself. I sucked in a breath at the sight.

"Hot damn, you're stunning," Brynn declared.

My face reddened, but I couldn't disagree.

My cinnamon-colored hair fell in loose waves around my shoulders and down to the middle of my back, where it met the crimson-colored lace corset that formed the top portion of my dress. The neckline was an elegant sweetheart shape, boosting my breasts up so they looked bigger than usual. At the waist, it billowed out widely, a masterpiece of tulle and lace.

"You look gorgeous," Miley admired, joining Brynn by the bathroom's entrance. "Did you ever figure out what the dress colors represent?"

"Yeah, I asked Anastasia about it. She said the red tonight is to represent finding my mate. The men will all be in masks and their demon forms for the first part of the night."

The women both raised their eyebrows.

"Shit. I forgot to mention the demon form thing, didn't I?"

"You did," Brynn agreed.

"They're bigger, covered in moving magical tattoos, and they have horns, wings, and tails. They shift when they feed, and when they lose control. They can do it on command too, but it makes them more... animalistic, I guess. Don't touch their wings or tails. I'm not sure about the horns, but I wouldn't touch them either unless you've asked."

"So avoid the winged guys," Miley summarized.

I smiled. "If you want to be safe."

"I have no desire to be safe." Brynn winked at me.

Miley sighed. "I'm going to spend all night trying to keep you from doing something stupid, huh?"

"No way. If you get between me and something stupid, I'll move you. Or he will, I guess."

Miles shook her head.

She had on a glittering, dove-gray dress that matched her eyes and fit the black-and-gray dress code the female guests other than me had been given. Her dark hair was pulled up in an elegant bun, a few curls hanging loose to frame her face.

Brynn wore a simple black silk dress that tied around her neck before flowing over her curves and to the ground. The simplicity of it made the light in her blue eyes stand out, and was absolutely stunning.

"Ready?" Miley asked me.

"I guess." I let out a long breath.

Brynn smiled. "It'll be great." She caught my hand and squeezed as I reached the door, and Miles pulled it open.

As we left the room, they pulled their masks on, both made of fabric that matched their dresses and covered the upper half of their eyes.

I would be the only one not wearing a mask, which was kind of stressful, but I'd survive.

WE REACHED the ballroom soon enough, and as I'd expected, Anastasia was waiting at the top of the massive staircase that led inside. She greeted both of my friends with hugs, not yet wearing her mask either.

Brynn and Miles headed down to join the party, while Anastasia and I slipped over to a balcony that let us look out at the party below.

Shit, it was breathtaking.

The room seemed to sparkle, with soft lights and candles positioned strategically so everyone could see, but not *too* well. It made the whole space look ethereal, and a soft layer of some sort of mist or fog floated through the room, adding to those vibes.

Soft instrumental music filled the air, played by a few performers dressed in gray and seated on a stage far to my left. Tables lined the room to the right, covered in food that smelled sweet from where I was.

A huge group of people moved and danced in the space, the grayscale colors of their clothing blending with the fog and adding to the atmosphere. Though I was expecting it, it still surprised me when I noticed the first demon, his dark pink wings standing out in the crowd.

After I saw him, I noticed another, with deep purple wings.

And another, with crimson.

And another, with violet.

There were so many of them, dancing, talking, and eating. Their wings and tails were all in shades of red, purple, and pink that should've looked ridiculous but were too damn magical. If I hadn't been used to Rafael's demonic form, I would've probably been nervous.

"Rafael warned me your sister-in-law might try something. I was ready when she showed up in a bright pink dress," Anastasia murmured to me.

I grimaced. "Classic Alena."

If the whole thing wasn't about demon traditions, I wouldn't have given a damn what anyone else wore. But clearly, with how particular they were being, their strange, over-the-top parties were important to them.

Anastasia's lips curved upward. "Your mother loaned her a black dress, thankfully. They'll both complain about it if you see them tonight."

"That's also classic for both of them."

She laughed softly, her eyes bright as she watched the dance below. "It's been a long time since I've had the pleasure of attending a mating celebration. There aren't many demons out there, and those of us who are unmated don't seem to have any desire to take a partner. So, thank you for giving me a reason to put this together, even if you did so unwittingly."

My eyes widened slightly, and I forced my gaze to remain on the crowd. "I don't know what you're talking about."

"One of my sons would've let it slip that Rafael was seeing you at some point, if you were truly together before he went to prison. I appreciate you being dedicated to keeping him safe, as well as free. Your secret is safe with me."

"The guys told me you wouldn't lie to your government for them," I admitted.

She smiled. "I would do anything I had to for them. I'd just rather they not know that, or they would ask me to bend the rules for them."

My throat swelled a little.

"They're good men," she said, her voice growing softer. "Very, very good men. Most demons wouldn't risk the wrath of our government to protect humans the way they do, and I respect them tremendously for it."

I nodded, though I was still uncertain about that.

Rafe and I were close, for the most part, but there were things we didn't really talk about. And his job was arguably the biggest.

"Rafael will treat you well for the rest of your life. If I had any doubt about that, I wouldn't have been looking for mates for my boys for so long. They don't realize how much happier they could be, and I want that for them."

"You're a good mom," I said quietly, but honestly.

"I've had a long time to learn." She took my hand and squeezed it lightly. "You remember how this works?"

"I just dance with every guy who asks, right?"

"Yes. After each dance, you kiss their forehead and take off their mask." She tapped the center of her head. "When you find Rafael, you kiss his mouth instead. When you dance with his brothers, if there's any question it might be him, simply try to drain a tiny bit of their magic. If you have anyone but your mate, it won't work, and you won't shift. Got it?"

"Got it," I agreed, though I didn't think I'd have any difficulties telling them apart. "How long is this party going to last?" The room was massive, and it looked pretty damn full. That meant there would be a lot of men to dance with.

"A *long* time. I'll bring you coffee when you start to look tired." She squeezed my hand one last time. "I'll tell them to close the doors. After I walk down the stairs, give it two minutes, and then follow me down. Eldrich will be waiting at the bottom, to ease you into it."

"Thank you." I squeezed her hand back.

"It's my pleasure." With one last wink, she swept off toward the large double doors. Her black dress sparkled around her as she walked.

The woman was so damn stunning.

I watched her float down the stairs, and when she got to the bottom, gave it what felt like two minutes.

Finally, I started my own descent.

The layers of my dress flowed with every step I took, and I lifted my head higher as the fabric moved lightly.

Putting my shoulders back the way I'd been told to—lectured to—a thousand times as a kid, I let one last, long breath escape me.

It was showtime.

fourteen

TATUM

ELDRICH WHISKED me onto the dance floor after a quick request, giving me a smile that reminded me so much of Rafael's, it made me smile too. Interacting with a man in his demon form outside of the usual stuff I did with Rafe was weird at first, but I adjusted quickly as I was spun around the room.

When every dance was over, I slid the man's red mask over his head and left a kiss on his forehead. That was weird at first too, but I got used to it.

Dancing with my brother was shitty, and it was awkward with my dad, but none of the dances were too long, thankfully.

I noticed Brynn off to the side of the room, talking with a huge guy in a red mask that wasn't a demon. He looked like... August, the dragon shifter.

She looked frustrated, from what I could see, but my dance partner whisked me away before I had time to think about it.

My mind was quickly dragged back to the guy I was dancing with.

At another point, I noticed Miley talking and laughing with a guy who wasn't in a demon form. He looked tall and strong, so I assumed he was a supernatural of some kind, but she looked happy. For her, that was huge.

When Rafael's first brother took my hand, I noticed his eyes lingering on someone across the room.

I followed them back to Brynn, who was no longer talking to the dragon shifter.

Taking stock of the man in front of me, with his stiff position and clean-cut hair, I decided he was Sebastian—though Rafael had told me I had to call him Bash, because we were family.

My mind went to my conversation with Anastasia, about being able to tell a man's potential mate apart from the crowd.

He wouldn't be able to look away from her.

We continued dancing, and his gaze moved every time we turned, his eyes lingering on my friend.

Could they be...

I opened my mouth to ask aloud, but the dance ended.

It was probably for the better. Sebastian wasn't looking for a woman to spend his life with; if he wanted one, he would've already gone looking for his potential mate in the city.

I removed his mask from his face and pressed a kiss to his forehead. He gave me a small, quick smile, followed by a shallow bow, and then strode across the room.

In the opposite direction from Brynn.

Maybe I had just been imagining the whole thing.

THE NIGHT WENT ON, and on, and on.

As promised, Anastasia brought me coffee at a few different points. When I told her my feet were killing me, she took my heels and told me to dance barefoot. I was too amused that my mother-in-law had stolen my shoes to protest.

I danced—and laughed—with Zander as he swept me around the room, spinning me too many times and making me grin even wider. Our dance went on longer than the rest, but I had no problem telling my mate from his brother, even in his demon form and mask. Zander's hair was longer and much more rumpled than Rafael's current cut, and he just seemed *wilder* than my mate and their oldest brother.

All night, I felt eyes on me. Rafael's eyes, everyone else's... I couldn't have told you whose they were, but I felt them constantly. I was technically the reason the party was happening at all, but still. It was a strange feeling.

The party's magic faded as the night went on, and I grew sweatier, annoyed with my dress, and tired of touching random men. There wasn't a way out, though, so I kept going.

It caught me off guard when I handed the last man his mask and a large, warm hand landed on my shoulder. Usually, the guys just tapped my arm or stepped in front of me.

My body relaxed immediately at the touch, and my lips curved upward automatically.

The man I'd just danced with strode into the crowd, and the one with a hand on my shoulder slid his hand down to mine, catching my fingers in his before spinning me to face him.

I stumbled, but he caught me smoothly, pulling me close. My chest met his, and his free hand found my lower back.

Rafael was in his demon form, which made my body flush. He lowered his head, and his lips brushed my ear. Goosebumps broke out along my skin at the contact, and I found myself leaning closer.

"You are the most stunning woman I have ever seen, Tater-tot," he murmured. "Even if you smell like an assload of other men."

A laugh escaped me, and he pulled me closer, brushing his lips over my cheek before pulling back enough to sweep me across the room.

I had learned enough about dancing as a kid to keep up with my partners for the most part throughout the night. But, with Rafael, it was simple.

Instinctual.

My body responded to the light pressure he put on my lower back. I turned when he wanted me to turn, and when he dipped me, it felt natural rather than scaring the shit out of me or catching me off guard.

When the dance neared its end, I noticed the music had gone quiet, and the whole room seemed to have gathered around us. My gaze found Anastasia, for the smallest of moments, and I saw tears in her eyes.

Emotion welled in my chest as Rafael dipped me one last time. His lips curved upward just a little, and he murmured, “Ready?”

“So ready,” I whispered back, earning a grin.

He eased me back to my feet, released me, and then swept in a low bow before straightening.

With a smile still on my face as well, I lifted my hands like I was going to slip his mask off—then grabbed his face, and kissed him.

The entire room erupted in cheers, the sound loud enough to shake the floor beneath our feet as Rafael kissed me back.

He pulled away after a moment, tossed his mask to the ground, then dragged me back into his arms and kissed me again, even more passionately. I gripped his suitcoat, holding on for dear life as the cheers continued until he finally broke the kiss again.

The devilish twinkle in his red eyes was fierce when he finally pulled away.

“What now?” I asked him, as the cheers finally began to fade. The party started to resume, with many more couples taking to the dance floor and the music growing louder again. I’d gotten the idea that demon parties could last all night, and I was too damn tired for that.

“Now, I take you back to our hotel room and make sweet, sweet love to you.” He plopped a kiss on my lips, and a laugh sputtered out of me.

I knew from the playfulness in his voice that he was joking, though the gleam in his eyes told me he definitely wouldn't protest if I was willing to go along with his plan.

"We should bring food with us."

"Knowing my mother, room service will arrive almost as soon as we do. We go now." He kissed my lips again, then winked at me.

More cheers erupted around us as he tossed me over his shoulder, and people hooted and hollered behind us as he carried me up the stairs and out of the ballroom.

Despite everything, I was grinning so broadly it almost hurt. The happiness in my chest was so thick, I could almost taste it.

I hadn't planned on anything that had happened with Rafael... but it had still changed my life.

And I could no longer deny those changes had been for the better.

MY EYES LINGERED on Rafael's ass and tail as he moved, both his hands on the backs of my thighs, even though I doubted he could feel them through the heavy layers of my dress.

He didn't set me down until we reached our room. Getting inside was quick, and then he put me on my feet with a flourish.

"So, what did you think?" He stepped around to my back and started undoing the laces on my corset. His fingers stumbled enough to make me think he hadn't done it many times before.

"It was kind of surreal at first," I admitted. "But the excitement faded, and then it just felt long. And sweaty."

He chuckled, slowly working his way through the laces. I could breathe deeper with every ribbon he loosened, so I felt better and better by the minute.

"What did you think? How many women did you dance with?"

"I didn't dance with anyone but you." His lips brushed my shoulder, lightly. "And truthfully, it took every shred of my control not to rip you away from every man who touched you. The urge to slit their throats was breathtakingly strong."

His lips brushed the back of my neck, and I shivered.

"Well, I'm glad you managed not to kill anyone."

He made a noncommittal noise. "Would've made the night move faster if I had. Your mom and Alena cornered me a few different times, and my mother had to make up excuses to untangle me from their grasps."

I laughed.

Maybe it made me a terrible person, but I was happy that he didn't fall all over them the way most people had throughout my life. My brother and Alena had been together since their freshmen year of high school.

"Your mother mentioned they've never seen *Coffee & Toffee*," Rafael said, his fingers moving back to the top of the corset and opening it much wider.

My body sagged, finally relaxing without the tight pressure of the dress. "They haven't. If they decide to come now, it'll be in an attempt to sway you to invest in something with them."

"I could destroy them, if you wanted me to." He slid the dress down to my waist, and I finally took a full breath in. "I've never had much of an interest in business, but Bash is good with it. We're involved in more markets than I care to think about; we could ruin them for you."

My lips curved sadly. He was being thoughtful—but that wasn't what I wanted. "I love them, in my own way. I don't want to see them hurt like that, or deal with the backlash of their anger. The best revenge for me is to succeed on my own, and to enjoy living my life. They've never really been happy."

"They don't deserve you." Rafael's lips brushed the side of my throat, and he slid the dress the rest of the way to the floor.

When I stepped out of it, his hands found my hips, and he stepped with me.

"They really don't," I agreed.

His lips brushed the top of my shoulder with another kiss, and I felt his gaze move slowly down my figure. His tattoo-covered hands slid up my torso, and I leaned against his chest as they teased my bare breasts.

"No bra?" He nipped at my ear.

"Nope." My eyes closed, and his fingers continued toying with my nipples.

"Are you going to let me drink your lust tonight, Tater-tot?" His tongue dragged over my earlobe.

We both knew he had already recovered from his time in prison. His skin had tanned to match his brothers, and his eyes never went red with hunger anymore. He'd recovered *weeks* earlier.

And yet, neither of us had brought it up.

Neither of us had put an end to the twice-daily feedings.

We both enjoyed it too much for that.

I couldn't have drank his lust that frequently if I tried, but as his brothers had told me, male demons were insatiable.

And shit, I definitely benefitted from that.

"You know I am, Riffraff." I pulled his hands off my chest, turning in his arms. When I started undoing his buttons, he effortlessly pulled his bowtie apart.

A knock at the door interrupted us, and I huffed.

His lips curved upward wickedly. "You said you were hungry."

"I changed my mind."

He clicked his tongue, and stepped away from me. When he reached the door, he glanced over and motioned for me to step to the side.

I must've been within view of the doorway.

Dutifully, I moved out of the way.

The door opened, and after a moment, closed again as Rafael rolled a cart of food inside.

"Tell me I'm brilliant," he drawled, with a sweeping gesture toward the food.

"You're brilliant. So is your mom." I strode up to the cart, my mouth watering when I saw the food. My horniness? Gone. Lust for the buttery steak in front of me had replaced it. "Strip down to your underwear and eat with me, Riffraff."

He didn't waste any time doing so, and we both grabbed our plates before collapsing on the bed together with them. I propped my back up against the headboard, and he sprawled out over the end of the bed, lifting my feet so they rested on his back while he was on his stomach.

I basically inhaled my food. While Rafael enjoyed his, he ate much slower. The bastard had probably been snacking throughout the party, while I had a belly full of coffee and nothing else.

His tail moved lazily through the air for a few minutes, making its way toward my feet. The warm length of it began slowly stroking up and down my ankles and calves, those rigid bumps dragging slowly over my skin and making my body warm.

"I'd like to hear more about your family life. We haven't talked about it much," Rafael said, as I cleared my plate.

"I don't like to talk about them much," I admitted. "I stay away from them for the most part. With how busy the coffee shop gets during the holidays, I have an excuse not to go home, too. Miles doesn't have any family left, so as you know, we always celebrate together. There's not much more to it than that. My brother bullied me, my parents helped him do it, and none of them respect me because I chose a different path."

His tail continued stroking my legs.

"I think there's more to it, Tater-tot."

"Like what?"

"Like the reason you glare at the luxury cars in the garage."

I sighed. "I guess I just don't like rich people after everything. It's not the money I mind—I don't give a shit about the money. It's all just a physical reminder of everything. I see an expensive car, or your fancy suits, and I feel like I'm stepping back into that world I hated. My life has been so much better since I escaped it, and I don't like feeling as if I'm being pulled back in."

His tail paused on my calf. "You don't like my suits?"

I grimaced. "It's not that I don't like them, I just..." I trailed off.

Rafael rolled onto his side, his tail tightening around my leg as he did. "Give it to me straight, Tatum."

I sighed. "I loved your joggers and your messy hair, that's all. I don't dislike that you're so pretty, and you dress nicely, and you're so charming, I just—you're grinning. Why are you grinning?"

He laughed. "You're really afraid to tell me that you don't like the way I dress."

"Well, it would hurt if you told *me* you didn't like the way I dress," I pointed out.

"I *don't* like the way you dress. I will always wish you would wear less clothing, Tater-tot." Somehow, he managed to say it with a serious expression.

A snort escaped me.

He grinned again, his tail resuming its motion. "I think your clothes are sexy, and I have no problem with them. I like that you're casual, and comfortable. I've been wearing suits for so long that it seems natural, but I'm much more invested in you being attracted to me. I'll start dressing more relaxed."

"You don't have to do that."

"Of course I don't. I want to." He leaned over and kissed my ankle before turning back to his nearly-empty food plate.

"What was your life like when you were a kid?" I asked him, growing curious.

"Happy," he said simply. "Really, really happy. The world was a very different place. Some supernaturals were at war, and others were in hiding."

When I asked for more details, he gave them to me readily. His tail kept stroking my leg, and when I finally ran out of questions, I felt the same way he had.

Happy.

And... I wanted more.

fifteen

TATUM

"IS YOUR TAIL EROGENOUS?" I asked Rafael. Though we'd touched each other plenty, we hadn't messed around with wings, horns, or tails before. Everything seemed more intense in demon form, so I avoided that.

"It is. Not as sensitive as my cock or wings, but sensitive. It's also uncontrollable for the most part. Damn thing has a mind of its own." It wrapped around my ankle, squeezing lightly.

I lifted my other foot and dragged it lightly over the length.

He growled, his body tensing. "Be careful, Tater-tot. I don't have nearly as much control as I should in this form."

"I know what I'm doing." I moved it lightly over his tail again, and a shudder rolled through him. "Have you ever let anyone touch your tail before?"

His mom had mentioned something about demonic forms being between mates.

"No. I didn't intend to take a mate, but I've always respected what is only meant to be shared with a life partner." His voice made my body warm.

"What about your horns?"

"You'll be the first."

"And your wings?"

His rumble was loud enough to make my lips curve upward. "They're yours, as you damn well know."

I did, but I wanted to hear him say it.

I ran my foot over his tail again, making him shudder. "How would you fuck me, if I asked you to tonight?"

He considered it while I teased his tail again. His wings were tucked in close to his back, but I'd play with them later.

"I would start by sliding those pretty little panties down, and tasting you. I've been dying to put my mouth on you."

Shit.

He turned around and sat up, his tail tightening on my ankle as he dragged a hand lightly over my free calf.

His fingers slid up and down my leg slowly. "I would stretch you with my fingers while I ate you out, so you were ready for me. And after you were desperate, I'd tell you to drink from me, so you'd shift. While you drank, I'd fill you with my cock, wrapping your tail in my hand so I had complete control of your pleasure.

My hips moved a little. I was drenched, my breaths were coming out quickly, and *shit*—I was done waiting.

He was perfect for me. I was perfect for him.

We were *mates*.

And we were going to be one in every way there was.

He was still stroking my leg, though I could imagine his hands were somewhere else. Somewhere higher, and wetter. "I'd make love to you, whispering about how sweet you felt wrapped around my cock. Telling you how much I love those perfect tits. Teasing your tail and stroking your wings until you shattered around me, and I filled you with my pleasure. When we were done, I'd start again. And again. And again. Until we'd both forgotten where you began and I ended."

I shuddered.

"You're absolutely dripping in lust, Tater-tot. Tell me what you want from me." His gaze was scorching. His hand had stilled on my calf, and I wanted it higher.

"Taste me." The command was foreign—usually, he was the one who set the pace and gave the orders.

But obviously, he wasn't going to make the first move on that.

His wings spread out behind him as he lowered his face between my thighs. With one sharp tug, my head hit the pillow and my back found the mattress.

He dragged my panties down to my thighs, leaned in, and inhaled deeply over my core.

I watched him, transfixed and turned on at the same time.

He opened my thighs wider with his hands, and then flicked his tongue over my clit.

No one had ever tried to go down on me before. I had never experienced anything like that, and I wanted *more.*

I cried out, hips jerking against his hold as his tongue worked me, slowly and lightly. My fingers found his horns, and I gripped the thick, hard spirals tightly, holding on for dear life as he ate me out.

My cries grew more frantic, my body's motions doing the same. When he slid a thick, warm finger inside me, I lost it.

I shattered on his face and hand, my movements desperate. He slowed but didn't stop as I came down from the high. When I pushed his head away a little, I got a red-eyed glower that dared me to stop him.

And I sure as hell wasn't going toe-to-toe with a demon who only wanted to bring me pleasure.

I rode out another climax as he stretched me with a second finger, and then a third. As the pleasure faded, my mind reeled, expecting him to be done.

He wasn't done.

If I wanted something else, I was going to have to say that.

So, I pushed his head away again. "I want more, Raf." The shortened version of his name slipped out, though I'd never used it before. "I want *you.*"

His eyes burned into mine. "You can't take my cock for the first time in this form, mate." He was bigger as a demon. So damn much bigger.

But considering the extra erogenous zones, and the fact that he shifted almost every time he ate, I was pretty sure his pleasure was more intense in his demon form, too.

"I can, and I will."

He snarled against my core, catching my clit between his teeth.

My hips jerked, more pleasure cutting through me. "Now, Raf. Give me your cock *now*, or this is over."

I didn't want it to be over.

I wasn't even sure I could stop him in that moment if I tried.

But he'd had his way for long enough.

His eyes were hot when he bit my clit again, holding on while my hips jerked and I fought a cry. As they slowed, he finally released me and lifted himself to a sitting position.

The man was massive.

He was absolutely, ridiculously stunning.

And I wanted him more than I could've ever imagined.

He tore my panties the rest of the way off, and his boxer-briefs followed.

My body thrummed with need when I saw his cock, thick and straining.

Straining for me.

"Tell me you want me," I said, as he lowered himself over me. His eyes were still red, and the heat of his body against mine was overwhelming.

"I've never wanted anything the way I want you, female." The head of his cock finally found my entrance. One of his massive hands slid up my bare abdomen, finding my breast and squeezing it.

His tail flicked my arm, and I grabbed it.

He swore, jerking his hips.

The head of him parted me, and I choked on air as the tip of him filled me.

My legs opened wider, my body tensing in response to his size.

He was too big.

There was no way.

I—

His hand left my breast, catching my cheek. He tilted his head back, and kissed me.

My body relaxed, and he slid another inch inside me.

I cried into his mouth, my hips arching, and he slid in deeper. His hand found my ass and tilted my hips.

"You wanted me, Tater-tot, and you have me. Feed, now." His command was so confident, I responded immediately.

I took in a shallow breath of his lust, and felt my body ripple.

A moan tore through me as I started to change, and he pushed in deeper.

"More, Tatum. *Now*. When you feel the shift, hold onto it."

I took in another breath of his lust, and when the shiver of change rolled through my body, I arched into it.

A cry escaped me as he slammed home, bottoming out inside me as my body softened to take him.

"You fit me perfectly," he growled, his hand sliding into my hair and moving over one of my horns. He thrust, and my hips moved to meet him, my body feeling as if it were no longer mine to control.

His thumb dragged over the tip of my horn, and I felt the pleasure roll all the way to my toes.

I gasped, and he tilted my head back again. His tail was still in my grip, so I dragged my thumb over the ridges, making him swear and move.

He thrust.

I arched.

And with his thumb on the sensitive tip of my horn, while mine dragged roughly over his tail, we climaxed together.

His snarls melded with my cries as we moved together violently, chasing the pleasure. His release was hot as he filled me with it, the sensation making my entire channel tingle.

"What did you do to me?" I moaned, my hips still moving lightly. Desperately.

I still wanted more.

Hell, I still *needed* more.

"I made you mine." He rolled me over in one smooth motion, his cock still buried inside me. The change of angle made my head spin, and I struggled to keep breathing with the thick pleasure of the sensation. "You're not sleeping tonight, Tatertot."

"I don't *want* to sleep tonight."

His hands found my wings, and I sucked in a breath.

My body shivered as he eased them open—the damn things spreading wide under his touch.

"I wanted to do this to you," I breathed, as he stroked the soft feathers lightly, lighting up every part of my body.

"Tomorrow."

I tightened around his cock as he touched my wings—and shattered again when he found the most sensitive spots. He went over the edge with me, roaring and flooding my channel with heat again.

"Holy shit," I moaned, hips rocking as I rode out the after-shocks of my pleasure.

"Drink from me," he ordered, his hands sliding down to my ass and squeezing.

I drank.

He did the same.

And we made love while we gorged ourselves on lust.

It was somehow both the sexiest moment of my life... and the most intimate as well.

WE MADE it into the shower together when an alarm went off on his phone. We had never gone to sleep, instead staying up all night to bring each other pleasure.

Both of us were sticky, and salty with sweat.

But we were practically glowing as well, and back in our human forms.

I had never imagined sex could be like that, and damn, I wanted more.

I must've said that aloud, because Rafael nuzzled my neck with his nose as the hot water fell over both of us. "The wedding's only a few hours. We'll get married, eat, dance a little, and then retreat."

"Deal."

Then his hands moved over my bare skin, washing me with soap, and I wanted more.

When I lined his cock up with my entrance, he lifted me off my feet and filled me from behind, pressing my tits to the wall. One of his hands worked my clit, and we both unraveled together a few minutes later.

"It still feels good as humans," I moaned to him.

"So damn good." He nipped at my neck, still buried inside me. "One more, and then you get ready."

He brought me back to the edge with his cock and fingers, and then finally pulled me off his erection, setting me back on my feet.

A fist pounded on our door while he lathered the soap between his hands. "Tatum? We have to get you ready," Miley called out.

Shit.

Rafael nuzzled my neck again, sucking lightly on my skin while I tried to gather the words to say.

I probably should've gotten some sleep. My brain wasn't quite working right.

My body sure as hell was, though.

“I’m in the shower!” I yelled back, sucking in a breath when he pinched one of my nipples. “Be there in five.”

“That’s not long enough,” Rafael murmured against my neck.

“Ten. Be there in ten!”

“Hurry up,” she hollered back. “We only have forty minutes.”

Shit.

Raf sighed against my throat.

“I’m hurrying!”

“We can do five,” he agreed, though clearly reluctant.

“The wedding is short, remember?” I reminded him.

He made a noncommittal noise, but went back to washing me.

I was wrapped in a complimentary robe and stumbling down the hall with a possessive arm on my hip a few minutes later.

Rafael left me in front of Brynn’s door with a searing kiss, waiting until Miley had tugged me inside before leaving.

sixteen

TATUM

"SO, DID YOU HAVE FUN?" Brynn asked, her voice low but her eyes bright. Miley was in the shower, and I'd dried my hair while Brynn got dressed. They were both a little hungover, but not too bad.

I lifted a shoulder. "The party was alright. I could tell it meant a lot to Anastasia, so it was worth it."

"Just alright? You haven't stopped smiling since you got here," Miley said from the shower.

I bit my lip, but couldn't defeat the smile. "I had fun after the party."

"You finally had sex?" Brynn demanded, her eyes even brighter as she stepped into the bathroom, buckling her bra behind her back.

"Maybe." I wasn't one for kissing and telling.

Brynn grinned. "If ever have a mate, I'm having sex everywhere. All the time. As much as possible."

"Then you should find yourself a demon." I paused. "Did I see you talking to the dragon shifter yesterday? You do know he's here trying to prove our relationship isn't real, right?" I had filled them in on the story and the vague answers they should give, since I was becoming something of a pro at giving those fake answers.

Did I like lying?

No.

Did I think it was necessary, given the situation?

Unfortunately, yes.

"I don't know what you're talking about." Brynn wouldn't meet my eyes.

"B," I warned.

"I already confronted her about it, and she wouldn't tell me anything. They look similar though. My theory is that he's one of her elusive, fabulous brothers," Miley said from inside the shower.

I blinked. "So your brother's a dragon, but you're not a supernatural?"

Brynn sighed. "I'd tell you everything if I could. There's magic preventing me from giving any details to people who don't already know them. Even among supernaturals, dragons are secretive. Ask Rafael; no one really knows anything."

I believed her.

I would ask Raf though, just because I was curious.

Just to have her back, I changed the subject. "So, did you two succeed at finding one-night-stands?"

Brynn shot me a grateful look. "Miles did."

"I will admit to nothing," she called.

"She was totally getting her flirt on with some guy. He wasn't a demon," Brynn said. "She only got back a few minutes before you, so if I had to guess, it was the best sex of her life."

"I regret telling you I've never enjoyed sex," Miley grumbled.

"Did that change?" I threw in.

Her answer was reluctant. "It did."

My lips stretched in a smile. "Is he human?"

"Too big to be human," Brynn said, shaking her head. "I was hoping he was a werewolf or a witch."

I made a face at the possibility of her hooking up with a witch, and Miley stuck her head out of the shower to do the same. "He's a vampire."

My eyebrows shot upward. "Did he drink your blood?"

Her face went red before she yanked it back into the shower.

I was a little worried, though, considering Raf and his brothers' occupation.

Maybe I'd text him to make sure he had invited vampires. I was sure they were friends with *some* of them; Raf had said from the beginning that not all vampires were good, or bad. "Is my phone in here?"

"You didn't have it when you came in," Brynn told me, combing her fingers through my hair. "Why?"

"No reason."

"He treated me way too well to be one of the shitty vampires Rafael and his brothers kill," Miley said, picking up where I had been going with that. "Don't worry about me. He said he's an old family friend."

It made sense. They would have family friends among all the different types of supernaturals.

But...

Well, I was still a little worried.

"Just be careful. Call me if you need anything."

Brynn snorted. "Because you're always accessible right now."

My face heated. "I'll get you guys Raf's brothers' phone numbers. I'll introduce you to them today, too. They would've told me if we were in danger, so I'm sure there's nothing to worry about. But I want you to be able to get in touch with them, just in case."

"I'm pretty sure I saw them. One of them, at least. He looks like Rafael, but grumpier," Brynn said, going to work on my hair with the curler. It would look much the same as it had the day before, but I liked it that way, so I was going with it.

"That would be Sebastian. He's the oldest. He's definitely the most serious one."

"Zander is the other one, right?"

"Yeah. I think he's the most adventurous one, and he's the youngest."

Brynn nodded. "It checks out." She glanced at the shower as Miley slipped out wrapped in a towel. "Do you have plans to turn your one-night-stand into a one-weekend-stand?"

Miley bit her lip to hide a smile. "Maybe."

Brynn grinned. "I'm happy for you."

"So am I," she admitted, before leaving the bathroom to get dressed.

"Who did you hook up with?" I asked her, knowing she'd gone into the party with wild plans.

Her lips twisted in a grimace. "No one. August snarls at every guy who looks at me. I'm going to single-handedly prevent you from getting caught in a lie just by being here."

I snorted, and she laughed too, though hers was tired. "Why is your brother so protective?"

"Dragons are obnoxiously possessive about *everything*. As far as my brothers know, I'm an innocent little virgin who sells coffee and candy with a smile."

"Most of that's accurate," Miley pointed out, grabbing a comb as she reentered the bathroom. She'd pulled on a pair of shorts and a loose tank top, not bothering with a bra.

"Right, but not the innocent part. I don't think they realize how much shit there is out in the real world." She continued working through my hair, and Miley turned me so she could do my eyeliner. "I'll never be able to fall in love like a normal person. They'd scare any sane human guy away in a heartbeat, and it's not like I interact with many supernatural beings."

My heart hurt for her. Miles and I knew damn well that Brynn was the romantic of the three of us. She wanted the flowers, the chocolates, the fancy dresses, the dates. It was no wonder she'd been so set on me introducing her to Rafael's brothers.

I couldn't help but think back to the way I'd seen Sebastian looking at her... but he could've been looking at someone else.

Or it could've been in my head.

I wouldn't get her hopes up over something that we had no control over. Maybe I'd figure out a way to ask him, after the parties were over, though...

"We'll be single together forever," Miles declared, as she and I both wrapped our arms around Brynn. She was the tallest of the three of us by far, but Miles was the shortest, so we always said they evened each other out.

"We should adopt a dozen cats," Brynn said.

"A dozen *dogs*," Miles corrected.

Brynn narrowed her eyes at Miley, and Miles narrowed hers right back.

"Six of each," I decided, grabbing the curling iron Brynn had set down for a moment.

Brynn stole it back, Miley picked up my makeup bag, and we finally focused on getting ready quickly.

I MET my dad at the top of the grand staircase shortly after that, staring down at the space below me.

The magical, foggy ballroom from the night before had been transformed into a dreamy human wedding venue in the hours since the party ended. The space was full of red roses and elegant chairs, with sweeping fabric in strategic locations.

"You look beautiful," my dad said, kissing my cheek.

Despite our rocky relationship, the compliment still made me smile.

"Work on that husband of yours during the honeymoon for me," he said with a wink. "We could use a business partner like him."

He wanted it to sound like a joke, but I knew he was completely serious.

I laughed, definitely not committing to that.

And... were we going on a honeymoon?

I didn't think we were.

If we were, Rafael hadn't mentioned it to me.

A stranger wearing a nametag gestured toward the staircase, giving us our cue.

We headed down the stairs, my hand tucked in my dad's elbow.

My gaze caught on Raf's as soon as we started, and when I saw his grin, I couldn't stop a smile of my own.

The whole thing was surreal... but not in a bad way.

Not anymore, at least.

The ceremony was brief, but sweet. Soon enough, we were declared husband and wife, and Rafael was kissing me.

Our massive crowd was led into a resort restaurant that had been reserved just for us, and we all took our seats. Raf and I had our own table, and when I saw Anastasia sitting with my family, she winked at me.

Gratitude swelled in my chest. The woman was a damn saint.

Bash and Zander were at the family table too, along with Brynn and Miley. It disappointed me when I noticed Sebastian wasn't staring at Brynn, a sign that she probably wasn't his potential mate.

I must've imagined him staring at her the night before.

Rafael's arm remained over my shoulder as we ate, and I leaned up against his side. I rolled my eyes but smiled every time he fed me a bite of his food or stole some of mine.

It was nice.

Really, really nice.

AFTER A NAP BREAK—DURING which I convinced Rafael to take my dress off me so I could *actually* nap—we all filed back into the ballroom. The new décor was similar to the way the wedding had been decorated, and classical music played.

Rafael and I chatted with the guests while other couples swept across the dance floor. When they asked questions I didn't have vague answers for, he would nuzzle my neck or drag his hands over my torso to make me blush, and lie like a pro.

It probably should've concerned me how easily he lied, but I trusted that he would tell *me* the truth.

After we were done greeting people, Anastasia put a bouquet of red roses in my hands and led me to the front of the room. I tossed it, and when I looked back, Miley was holding the flowers. Her face was red, and I saw her eyes flick toward the side of the room.

Something told me her new vampire guy was over there.

After Rafael and I ate a few of the desserts, he was pulled onto the dance floor for a mother-son dance. The father-daughter one followed, too.

We fed each other cake after that, and yes, smashed it all over each other's faces. And after *that*, came the garter toss.

Anastasia dragged Zander and Bash to the forming crowd of men for that one. Rafael pulled it down my leg with his teeth, and winked at me before he threw the elastic over his shoulder.

I had a perfect view of his brothers as the garter flew toward them. It was zooming straight toward Bash, but he side-stepped it at the last second. Zander followed him—and got hit square in the face with the fabric.

I snorted, and Rafael laughed.

We danced together a few more times before sneaking out. The party would last until the early hours of the morning, but neither of us was interested.

We spent a few hours in bed together, then slept like rocks until lunchtime the next day, when we went to the beach before getting ready for yet another party.

THE DRESS for Saturday was a rosy pink color. According to Anastasia, the color represented adjusting to the bond. I got ready with Miley and Brynn again, and found Miley blushing even more about her vampire.

Brynn was still being cock-blocked by her brother the dragon shifter, but she seemed to be having a good time anyway.

Sunday, we spent even more time at the beach, which was a blast. For the final party, I wore black, to represent the permanence of the bond.

We said our goodbyes the next morning, and then flew out to a different beachfront resort halfway across the world.

Snuggling against Rafael's side on another airplane, it finally hit me that what we had wasn't going to change. We were together, for better or worse, no matter what. When shit happened, we would have to work it out together, instead of splitting.

I wasn't sure whether to be excited or nervous about that, though the sex was leading me toward the first option.

I kept feeling like the bubble of bliss we'd formed was going to pop—and a few days after we left, it finally did.

WE WERE MAKING out in the private jacuzzi on the front porch of our cabana when my phone rang. I ignored it, until it rang again.

No one ever called me twice.

Disentangling myself from Rafael, I padded across the porch, into the sand, and to the lounge chair I'd left it on.

Brynn's name was on the screen, so I lifted it to my ear.

"Hello?"

"Something's wrong," she said quickly, enough panic in her voice that I immediately went on alert.

"What happened?"

"Miley didn't come home last night. I figured she just stayed with Evan, but she didn't answer when I texted. Or when I called. I gave it a few hours, and then tracked her phone and hunted her down. I found it in a dumpster, along with the clothes she was wearing yesterday. They're covered in blood."

My eyes widened. "What the hell? Where is she? Is she okay?" The words flew from my lips, though I knew Brynn didn't have answers for them.

"I don't know. I don't know what to do. I can't ask my brothers; they're not allowed to get involved. I don't know if I should call the Villins, or—"

Rafael took the phone from me, tapping the button to put it on speaker. His hand landed on my hip, his chest to my back as he held it between us and repeated my question. "What happened?"

Brynn told the story again, and Rafael's eyes narrowed as he listened. "Who is Evan?"

"He's a vampire. She met him at your party. She said she was falling in love with him, and Miley never gives guys a chance. I—"

"Evan what?"

Brynn was silent for a moment. "I don't know his last name," she finally said.

He looked at me, and I shook my head.

Miles had been tight-lipped about him.

"I'll call Bash and Zander. Tatum will text you the code for the apartment next door to ours; I own it. Let yourself in and stay there until someone from my family comes for you." Rafael gave the orders smoothly. While there was authority in his voice, there was warmth too. People listened to him, and I understood why they did.

"I don't want to hide," Brynn protested.

"My family has made a lot of vampires very, very mad. This was a targeted attack, and we don't want anyone else going after you. Go to our apartment, where we can keep you safe until we understand what and where the threat is."

Brynn's voice was small when she said, "Okay."

"I love you, B. We're going to figure this out," I added quickly. "Miles is going to be fine."

She whispered her agreement, and Rafael hung up the phone.

"She *is* going to be fine, isn't she?" I asked him, fear rolling through my stomach.

Raf held my gaze for a long moment before he said honestly, "I don't know."

And then, he launched into action. The man guided me to the couch in the front room of our bungalow, then moved so quickly I had a hard time following him with my eyes. He talked to his brothers while he packed our bags and straightened up the room, and stayed on the phone while he typed on his laptop for a few minutes.

When he continued working as a car arrived to take us back to the airport, I put together something I should've realized much, much sooner.

Rafael's world was much bigger than mine.

His *life* was much bigger than mine.

Our relationship was only a small blip for him, but it was huge for me.

He had an entire life before the one we'd shared... and it didn't fit together with mine.

Not at all.

And I had no idea how we were going to deal with that.

Or rather, how *I* was going to deal with that. Because clearly, Rafael had decided not to tell me that my friends and I were at risk because of his job.

If Miley was hurt because of Raf, I would never forgive him for that.

Brynn and Miles were the family I had chosen, and I would fight with everything I had for them.

Even if it cost me my mate.

seventeen

RAFAEL

THE FURTHER WE got from the cabana we'd been staying in, the more Tatum shut down. I could see it in her eyes and her responses to me.

When I touched her, she pulled away.

When I reached for her, she moved.

When I asked her something, her answers were short and clipped.

I dreaded her response when she found out what had likely happened to Miley. Vampires didn't *kill* when humans were involved and they wanted revenge. They knew it was far crueler to turn them.

A vampire would battle bloodlust through their entire existence, assuming they were free. And if they *weren't* free, it was effortless torture to turn a human and then let them starve to death, slowly turning to stone.

I knew the pain of that better than most.

Halfway through the flight back to Scale Ridge, I got a message from Zander. It was only two words:

ZANDER

Found him

I forced my breathing to remain even as I waited for another message, so Tatum wouldn't look over and realize we'd learned something.

The message was to me and Bash. I knew Bash was out on the streets, separate from Zander. We'd been looking for the headquarters of the volatile vampire clan that had moved into Scale Ridge around the time I escaped prison.

I was much more useful pounding pavement with Bash. That hadn't been an option with August on my ass, looking for evidence that I was going to return to killing rogue vampires. As soon as he was gone, I would be at it again.

The notification lit up my screen again.

ZANDER

Evan is working for Eric Reiner. He's a young, born vampire, and was never registered. His dad is Charlie Deel, and he looks almost identical to the old man. He convinced Charlie to let him go to your party in his place.

ME

Fuck

Charlie was an old friend of my parents, and the head of one of the only vampire clans that actively worked with me, my brothers, and our dad to keep the vamps in line.

Eric Reiner's sister's death was what landed me in prison. Stories of her cruelty to humans had circulated for centuries, but we didn't go after her until we had the evidence to prove it. It had taken nearly a hundred years to gather, but we had it. When we were caught, we handed it over, too.

It just hadn't mattered to our government.

She was ancient, with too many friends.

BASH

I followed the blood from the dumpster into the office building it was behind. It's still just as clear as the last time I walked through it. They've improved how well they hide from us, or they're not here.

ME

Have we gotten underground yet?

ZANDER

Still working on that. Stay tuned.

I ran a hand through my hair.

Tatum had no plans to accept that part of my life. She wasn't going to embrace the fact that I worked with my brothers to protect humans from vampires.

And I had no idea what to do about that.

She glanced over at my phone at the same time another text came through.

BASH

Have you warned Tatum that Miley might have been turned?

The blood drained from Tatum's face, and her gaze pierced me a heartbeat later. Her voice was low and flat as she said, "Explain that. Now."

I was going to hell.

I had booked a private plane to Scale Ridge so we could get there sooner, so we had all the privacy we needed. I just wasn't looking forward to screwing with our dynamics any more than I already had.

"Some vampire clans have twisted ideas of revenge. They'll turn humans that supernatural beings are close with, and starve them. They'll usually let the new vampires turn permanently to stone, unless the supernaturals give them what they want."

"What do they want?"

"I think you know the answer to that, Tater-tot." I tried to brush a few strands of hair off her cheek, but she lifted her hand, catching my wrist to stop me.

"Don't touch me. You lied to me—you've been lying to me for months." She released my wrist, knowing I wouldn't touch her without her permission.

"I've never lied to you. You didn't ask questions you didn't want answers to, and I didn't give answers to questions you didn't ask." I forced myself not to react to the fear growing in my abdomen.

If her friend died, she wouldn't forgive me.

She would do whatever it took to make sure we lived our lives as separately as possible, knowing it was the opposite of what I wanted.

It would kill me to stay away from her after so much time at her side.

"Don't try to pin this on me," she hissed. "I didn't keep secrets. You did."

"You made it clear how you felt about my job; I wasn't going to spout facts about how many vampires wanted me dead."

"I deserved to know that my friends and I were in danger, no matter how uncomfortable it made you to tell me. We would've been careful. We would've been suspicious. Instead, we were excited that Miley finally found a guy who could make her feel good. She never feels good—she's always stressed about everything. I could've protected her just by talking to her, but now I'm the reason she's gone." Her voice cracked with the last bit, and she wiped violently at a tear that escaped.

Guilt had my jaw clenching.

She was right.

And she deserved an apology.

"I'm sorry, Tatum. If I could go back, I would warn you. We had cameras and men trained on your friends; you weren't sitting ducks. We didn't predict this, and weren't prepared for it, and I'm sorry. I should've told you"

"What? They had security guards?"

"My brothers tracked your phone to your apartment the day I met you. We've been in the business long enough to know that if we can, our enemies can too. Bash and Zander had security lined up for Miley and Brynn before they ever met you. You might not like our job, but we're damn good at it."

"Then how did this happen?" Her voice trembled a little, and she wiped away a few more tears.

It took effort not to drag her into my arms and hold her to my chest.

I explained the situation with Eric, and Charlie's son. She leaned further into her chair as my explanation went on.

Tatum groaned when I finally finished. "This is a damn mess, Raf."

She was using my nickname.

That was a good sign.

"Immortality is messy," I said simply.

"Your reasoning is shitty."

"I know it is."

We were both quiet for a few minutes. When she spoke again, her voice was barely above a whisper. "Do you think Miles is still alive?"

"Yes." I didn't hesitate, and it wasn't a lie. "The vampires want me and my brothers. They'll probably turn her, and send a ransom video in the next twelve to twenty-four hours. They'll want a trade; me, for Miley. If we can't figure out a way to get her back without it, we'll go through with the trade."

Tatum lifted her hands to her forehead. "How do you live your life like this? I feel like I'm going to have a mental breakdown."

"We break down when we need to—and then we keep going, because it's the only choice we have."

"It's not the only choice. You could walk away. You could live a normal life, or whatever the equivalent is for a demon."

"Saving humans' lives is worth a hell of a lot more to me than fucking my way around the world, Tater-tot. I'm sorry it doesn't make sense to you, but that is the damn truth."

She shook her head. "Add me to the text conversation with your brothers. I want to know everything, Raf. If I find out you're keeping *anything* else from me, we're done. You and I can both starve to death for all I care." With that, she stood and crossed the jet's living space without an explanation, closing herself in the single bedroom it boasted.

I let out another long breath.

I had screwed up everything between us… and I didn't know if there was a way to fix it.

If there was, I wouldn't have a chance to find it until after Miley was safe again.

And when she was, it looked like there was a damn good chance I'd be gone.

eighteen

TATUM

BRYNN THREW her arms around me in a fierce hug the moment I stepped through the apartment's doors. Tears I'd been holding back for too long stung my eyes, and I gripped her just as tightly.

"Zander won't tell me if he thinks she's alive," Brynn said, letting go with one hand so she could wipe her own tears away with the back of it. "Did Rafael say anything?"

The bastard had said a lot of things.

"He thinks they turned her into a vampire to torture her with bloodlust, and that they're going to offer to trade her for Raf," I admitted.

She deserved the full truth as much as I did, if not more.

"Way to break the news gently," someone muttered. When my head jerked upward, I found Zander sitting on a cushy couch, his fingers moving rapidly over his laptop's keyboard. There were two other laptops open, one on each side of him, but he wasn't paying them any attention at the moment.

"Shit." Brynn wiped away more tears. "I should call my brothers. They probably can't do anything, but... I should call them."

"Dragons are possessive. Call them, and there's a good chance they'll take you so far from here, you won't find out what happens to Miley," Zander said absentmindedly, fingers still flying on the keyboard.

"I hate that he's right. Where's Rafael?"

"In his apartment, packing my shit." I pushed a few strands of greasy hair out of my eyes. There hadn't been time to shower before we left paradise, and I needed to clean both sand and a little sunblock out of it.

The clicking of Zander's keys paused.

Brynn's eyes widened. "What? Why?"

"I can't trust him. He didn't tell me we were in danger, and now it's my fault that Miley's probably in pain right now."

Zander's keys didn't resume clicking.

"I didn't even know he owned this apartment—the bastard obviously doesn't trust me, either." I strode into the kitchen, hunger clenching my stomach.

It messed with me a little, seeing the apartment that was so similar to mine and Raf's, but so different too. The floorplan was exactly the same, but reversed. The colors were lighter—the cabinets were white, the floors were a light natural wood, and the furniture was softer. It lacked the hard edges and contrast I loved about our apartment.

When I opened the fridge, the damn thing was empty.

My phone vibrated in my pocket, and when I pulled it out, a text showed on the screen.

RAFAEL

I ordered food. Should be here in ten. If you want your things, you can come in here and get them yourself.

My nostrils flared.

ME

You said you would handle the packing.

RAFAEL

Changed my mind. I'm not going to help you leave me.

I shut the fridge door a little too hard.

"Apparently, Raf ordered food. Can I borrow some of your clothes?" I asked Brynn.

She didn't ask why. "Go ahead. I took the room on the left of the stairs. The right one is for Miles, if..." she trailed off, and her eyes watered.

Mine did too.

I pulled her in for another hug. "*When* she gets back."

"*When* she gets back," Brynn whispered. "I'll come with you. I'm tired of being alone with Zander. He doesn't answer any of my questions."

He snorted, but didn't say anything else.

She scowled in his direction, holding my arm as we walked toward the stairs.

"Safe to say you're not potential mates?" I asked, attempting a joke.

Her nose wrinkled. "No. We've spent the last twelve hours together, and he already feels like another brother."

"I heard that disdain," he called out.

"I already have too many brothers," she shot back, and then looked at me. Her voice was soft when she asked, "Are you really leaving Rafael?"

"Yes." My voice was confident, until I actually pictured myself walking into our apartment and packing my shit. "No." My voice wavered. "I don't know. It hurts, knowing how many things he kept from me."

She squeezed my arm, where she was holding it. "I'm sorry."

"Me too. I wish Miles wasn't hurting because of me. I feel like shit for that."

"They might not turn her," Brynn said in a small voice.

"From what Raf said, I think it's inevitable. What if she hates me for what happens? What if her hunger drives her mad? What if—"

Brynn squeezed my arm again. "Don't lose yourself in the what-ifs. Out of all of us, Miles is the most rational and capable. Whatever happens, we'll figure it out. If she hates you, we'll woo her back with chocolate."

"You know she rarely eat my chocolates," I tossed back.

"With blood, then. We've both got plenty of that." She gave me a small smile, and I couldn't help but return it.

Brynn sat on the toilet while I slipped into the shower.

"What do you know about vampires?" I asked.

"Not much. I really don't interact with supernaturals except my brothers, and you guys are always with me. You know I don't see them all that often."

I nodded even though she couldn't see me, as I started to wash my hair.

"Do you think Rafael will answer all of our questions about them if we ask?" she wondered.

I hesitated. Part of me wanted to say no, just because I was still hurt and pissed off. But honestly... "Yes," I admitted. "I told him if he kept anything else from me, we were done for good. I think he believed me."

"Did *you* believe you?"

"I don't know." I closed my eyes, letting the hot water roll over me. "I think I do. I trusted him, before. Part of me still does. If he lies again, or hides anything else, that part will be gone. I don't know where we could possibly go from there." After a pause, I asked her quietly, "How long do you think it'll be until she lets someone in after this?"

"Too long." Her words were barely above a whisper. "I wish they had targeted me instead. She'll survive the hunger... but it'll take her time to get there. At least I know my brothers would be there, if it was me. They'd teach me everything there is to know, even if they had to knock a few heads in to do it."

"We'll have to be your brothers for her, then."

"We've got this." There was doubt in her voice, and I laughed softly when I heard it. She did too. "I'll work on the confidence. By the time we get her back, I'll be ready."

"We both will be." I finished up in the shower, dried off, and then pulled on a sleep shirt Brynn had grabbed from her room.

When we stepped out of the bathroom, I heard Rafael's voice downstairs, and stopped in my tracks.

Brynn grabbed my arm again and pulled me down the stairs, whispering, "Hiding isn't going to get you anywhere."

I made a face at her, and her lips curved in a small smile.

Rafael was on the phone in the kitchen when we made it down, and he ended his phone call as we went straight for the takeout food. He'd ordered from what he knew was one of my favorite places; obviously, he was trying to soften me up.

It wasn't going to work.

Brynn grabbed plates and silverware, and I carried the bags to the kitchen table. Rafael followed me. His hand brushed my hip so lightly, I wasn't sure whether he'd actually touched me, or I just imagined it.

Goosebumps broke out on my arm anyway. It had been almost ten hours since he last touched me... not that I was keeping track.

"We need you to tell us everything about vampires," Brynn told Rafael bluntly, as she dished food onto her plate.

Raf took my plate and started filling it. When I tried to take it back, he shot me a warning look, and I sat back down. I wanted to argue with him about it, but I knew if I did, it would take longer to get to his explanation about vampires.

The bastard was still going to insist on taking care of me, like he had at the resorts.

"Vampires are very similar to demons, but they function on blood instead of lust. They have a vampire form, and the men are insatiable, like male demons. Unlike demons, a vampire sating their hunger can get violent, given that blood is involved. If they're careful, feeding causes no pain and actually brings pleasure to whoever they're drinking from."

Rafael set my plate down in front of me and started filling his own. "The biggest difference is that vampires can be made by draining a human's blood while they have vampire blood in their system. The vampires we hunt and kill are those who turn humans without reason, and those who feed violently enough to maim or kill the humans they've fed from. Without someone keeping them in line, there would have been many more deaths. A vampire without control can kill a dozen humans a day without batting an eye."

I fought the instinct to raise my eyebrows.

A dozen humans a day?

He definitely hadn't mentioned that bit when he was explaining it to me, and I was calling him a murderer.

"Damn. You guys are heroes, then." There wasn't any sarcasm in Brynn's voice, just respect. "Why did they throw you in jail?"

He rehashed his story about the ancient vampire woman they had killed, and how he'd taken the fall for it so his brothers could walk free.

"And August is watching you to make sure you *don't* kill more vampires?" Brynn's eyebrows were raised high in her forehead.

"Dragon shifters are neutral when it comes to human and supernatural conflicts. They don't respect humans the way demons do, because they don't need you," Rafael said simply.

Her eyebrows dropped, and her gaze did too.

We all ate in silence for a minute, until I spoke up. "Do dragons have human mates sometimes, too?"

Raf looked at me, his gaze unreadable as it slowly moved over my face. "I don't know."

"You don't know?"

"As you've gathered from Brynn, dragon shifters are secretive. I've heard legends of a place deep in the Scaled Mountains, past the prison, where they take their mates. It may or may not be accurate. Most stories don't have a name for it, and just call it *Mate Mountain*."

Brynn's gaze snapped back to him, her eyes wide.

She didn't say a word, but something told me he was right.

Mate Mountain totally existed.

She went back to her food, and when he looked back at me, he winked.

Winked.

As if I wasn't still pissed at him.

I fought the urge to flip him off. Instead, I changed the subject and focused on my food at the same time. "What's the plan to get Miles back?"

"Bash just headed out to follow a lead I got while I was on the phone a few minutes ago," Rafael said.

My attention jerked back to his, much like Brynn's had, my eyes narrowed.

"You'll see the texts between us on your phone, next time you pick it up." He finally took a bite, chewed, and swallowed.

I ignored the desire to pick up my phone and check. I'd do it when he wasn't watching, to make sure he was telling the truth.

"If this lead is as promising as we think, I'll go out tonight to drag Eric out of the woodwork. He still hasn't sent a ransom, so we assume he's waiting for us to find him."

"Is that safe?" I asked, before I could consider the words, or the worry.

"Safe enough. I'll have a dragon shifter tailing me, and even a Reiner in mourning isn't stupid enough to kill a Villin with a dragon watching."

"That doesn't sound like a guarantee."

"There are no guarantees in our world outside of mate bonds, Tater-tot." He took another bite.

I watched his jaw move, and his Adam's apple bob as he swallowed.

Did the man have to be so damn attractive?

"What happens to a demon if their mate dies?" Brynn asked.

I froze.

Rafael continued eating. "Mates live or die as one."

"All supernatural beings do," Zander put in from where he sat on the couch. "When souls are bound, they're bound permanently."

"No one is going to die," I said, forcing myself to take another bite of my food. "And if our lives are tied together anyway, Rafael isn't going to meet any vampires without me."

"I won't walk you into a room full of vampires who want revenge on me." Raf's growl was immediate, his usually-smooth voice harsh. "Not a fucking chance."

"Then you're not walking into it either." I took another bite.

He set his fork down. "That's not your call, Tatum."

Zander's computer made a noise, and he called out, "Reiner's on the line."

All of us were rushing across the room before he'd even finished speaking.

Zander hit a button, pulling up the video call and blocking his camera with a sticky-note at the same time.

Brynn and I made strangled noises when Miley appeared on the screen, her eyes glowing red and her skin spotted with dried blood. She looked even thinner than usual, yanking wildly against metal chains that had been locked around her wrists. All she had on was a sports bra and a pair of lounge shorts, her body was covered in the same magical tattoos we had in our demon forms, and her feet were *gray*. The gray seemed to be spreading up her legs, too.

Raf pulled me to his chest, and I couldn't help but wrap my arms around him, clinging to him for support. He held me close, lifting a finger to his lips to tell me and Brynn to be quiet.

The call cut off a moment later, and a text came through.

UNKNOWN

Your mate for her friend.

Rafael snarled at the message, and Zander's shoulders tensed.

An address came through a moment later, and Zander was immediately on the phone.

Bash answered just before it went to voicemail. "What do you want? I think I finally found them."

"We have an address; I just sent it to you. They want Tatum."

A moment passed. "I was right; I'm at the address you sent. I'll look around before I head back to help with a plan."

"Be careful," Brynn blurted.

A moment of silence passed.

Her face went pink, her eyes still flooded with tears from seeing Miley.

Finally, there was an awkward, "I will," on Bash's end before the call disconnected.

nineteen

TATUM

BRYNN and I sat on the couch, gripping each other's hand tightly while Rafael paced the living room like a trapped animal. Across the couch, Zander's fingers flew over his laptop's keyboard as if the man was possessed.

Bash finally stepped into the apartment. It was only an hour and a half after the phone call, but it felt like a lifetime had passed.

His gaze went immediately to me and Brynn, and his shoulders relaxed a tiny bit. "They've set up shop at the new nightclub on Deck Street."

"Should've known," Zander muttered.

"The security is beefy. We won't get past without raising an alarm. Not before Miley turns completely to stone."

Brynn's grip on my hand tightened painfully. Mine on hers probably did too.

"We go in together, then," Rafael said.

"All of us." Sebastian was still looking at me and Brynn.

"Me too?" Brynn whispered.

"No." His answer was swift, and harsh. "You're not one of us."

Her eyes flooded with more tears, and his gaze darkened.

"It wasn't an insult. You're safe because you're not a Villin," Zander said, finally closing his laptop and setting it down on the couch. He did the same with the other two, and then looked at me and Brynn. "Her feet were stone, and it was spreading up her legs. That means no one has fed her since she's turned. The pain will be excruciating—and it will kill her in less than a day if we let it."

"I thought it takes years for vampires and demons to starve to death," I said.

"Healthy ones. A new vampire is much more fragile."

Shit.

I squeezed my eyes shut. "When do we leave?"

"You're not going anywhere. I won't risk your life," Rafael growled back.

"They want her. They won't let us in without her," Zander countered. "She's a Villin now. We'll keep her safe."

Raf snarled again.

I was going to have to talk to him.

Despite me being angry and hurt, I still knew he would listen to me. He would have a conversation about it, even if he wouldn't with anyone else.

I squeezed Brynn's hand one last time before letting go and standing up. Rafael's eyes were narrowed as I stepped up to him and took his hand. His grip on me was even tighter than Brynn's had been. "We'll get ready and be back in a few minutes."

"Take your time. We need to get backup into place and work out a few other things before we head out," Bash said.

I towed Raf out of the apartment. His jaw was clenched so tightly, I could almost hear his teeth grinding. Typing the code in only took a moment, and the door unlocked and opened smoothly.

Rafael shut it behind us. He remained in front of it, his back to the entrance as if that would keep me from leaving. "I won't risk you getting hurt, Tater-tot."

Arguing wouldn't get me anywhere when he was that against it. Honestly, arguing never got me *anywhere* with him. Having an honest, logical conversation was the only way to reach a decision we were both comfortable with.

So I stepped up closer to him and put my hands on his chest.

His lifted to my lower back, and pulled me closer.

"Miley is my family," I told him simply. "You have Zander and Bash; I have Brynn and Miles. She's alive, and she's hurting. If Bash or Zander were in her place, I would do whatever I had to, to get them out. I need you to do the same for me."

He closed his eyes, jaw clenching again.

I remained where I was, giving him time to think, process, and decide what he was going to do.

Rafael was far from stupid. He knew that it wasn't just a decision about rescuing my best friend. The choice he had to make was either to risk my life to save Miles, or to lose me by letting her die.

"You don't leave my side for anything," he finally gritted out, opening his eyes. His stare was hard, and serious. "We maintain physical contact the entire time we're there."

I nodded. "That's fair."

"If I give an order while we're there, you follow it. If I hide you somewhere, you stay until I'm back. And if I tell you to shift and run, you shift and run."

I nodded again. "Understood."

He let out a long breath and then released me.

I was still hurt, and angry, but I wrapped my arms around his neck anyway. He hugged me tightly, and I buried my face in his neck. "Thank you, Raf."

A moment passed, and I released him. He let go of me, his sharp gaze following me as I stepped back. "We need to dress for a nightclub, right?"

He was already wearing slacks and a light blue button-up rolled to his elbows, so he was ready.

Rafael dipped his head in confirmation.

I had already put on my black, glittery bralette and was struggling to zip up the matching mini skirt when Raf met me in the closet, my tiny makeup bag in his hand. His eyes moved over me quickly, and the barely-there lust coming off him grew more vibrant.

"Turn." He tucked the makeup pouch beneath his arm.

I reluctantly turned.

He held the stiff fabric together with one hand and worked the zipper up with the other. "When did you get this?"

"Brynn told me and Miles she needed us to go dancing with her a few years ago, and made us buy clothes for it. We went to a nightclub, and she *hated* it. It was so loud and crowded, we only lasted twenty minutes. When we got home, she turned on music and we had our own dance party in the kitchen."

I bit my cheek, fear for my friend swelling in my stomach again.

What if we couldn't get to her?

What if they succeeded at killing us?

What if—

Raf's lips brushed my shoulder, lightly, as he finished zipping up the skirt. "We'll get her back and make it home in one piece, Tater-tot." His voice was still quieter than usual, but its smoothness had returned.

"I really, really hope so," I whispered.

His lips brushed my shoulder again, and I leaned my back against his chest. He slid a hand over my very-exposed midriff, and his chest rumbled lightly. "If the situation was different, I would be driving you to a store for an outfit that covered a little more of you."

"If the situation was different, I would refuse to change until you convinced me to stay home and get naked with you, just so I didn't have to go to a nightclub."

His lips were curved upward slightly as I turned around and plucked my makeup bag from his hand.

He leaned against the doorway, watching me put makeup on for all of a minute and a half. When I left it on the counter, I took his arm, and we walked down the stairs together.

I was still pissed at him, but my anger would have to wait until Miles was safe. After that, I would figure out if I trusted him enough to continue sharing my life with him.

If not... well, I wasn't going to think about that until I had to.

BASH AND ZANDER were ready when we got back to the other apartment. I gave Brynn a hug, then followed the guys to the elevator.

"What's the plan?" I asked them, as it descended toward the parking garage.

"Get in. Get out with Miley. Stay alive." Zander spouted the facts.

My eyebrows shot upward. "There's no plan?"

"We don't have time to plan," he said bluntly. "There's no guarantee they're even keeping her there. But it'll take my team a few days to break into the club's cameras, and Miley doesn't have a few days. We're going in blind."

We stepped out of the elevator and followed Bash to his vehicle. It was a massive Hummer, with shiny black paint. The glass looked thicker than most, which made me think it probably had more than a few safety upgrades. From what I knew of Bash, it seemed reasonable to assume he drove around in something that was basically a well-disguised tank.

Raf and I took the back seat, and Bash pulled out of the garage as I drawled, "Write that on my headstone. *There was no plan.*"

Rafael's chest rumbled in warning.

He didn't like talking about me dying, and not just because it meant he would die too.

Bash intervened. "You and Rafe will hold Eric's attention. Zander and I will go through the building until we've found Miley or determined she's not there. Whoever finds her will haul her out. Whichever of us doesn't have her will rejoin you, we'll kill Reiner, and we'll get out. If August has a problem with it, he can drag *my* ass to prison this time."

I brushed a few strands of hair from my eyes. It was still a little damp, and probably didn't look fantastic, but I didn't care. "That sounds better than going in blind, at least."

"We'll be fine." Zander reached back to pat me on the knee, but Raf batted his hand away.

"Our people have been slowly slipping into the club with tonight's normal crowd. They'll keep an eye out for us so no one can kill us while our backs are turned," Rafael told me. "And remember—"

"I don't leave your side. I know. I agreed to it."

He only looked a little satisfied by the answer. Considering that we were about to walk into a nightclub full of vampires who wanted us dead, I didn't blame him.

BASH PARKED HIS TANK—I mean Hummer—in the parking lot alongside all the normal cars. It stood out like a sore thumb, but he didn't seem to give a damn, just locking it and tucking the key in his pocket.

Scale Ridge didn't have much crime, so it was probably safe. And something told me that anyone who tried to break in would regret it.

Rafael wrapped an arm around my waist, his hand landing on my hip as all four of us strode toward the doors of what looked like a huge warehouse. The noise of the music playing inside grew louder as we approached, and I tried not to grimace.

What little experience I'd had told me I really wasn't into nightclubs.

The guys didn't bother waiting in line, and when the bouncers at the door saw us, they waved us through without pause.

It occurred to me that Bash and Zander had probably been there before. Rafael had been in prison, but as far as I knew, Zander and Bash were living in Scale Ridge the whole time. Living there meant eating there, and Raf had told me they preferred to feed in public places like nightclubs, to make that part of their lives easier.

Rafael's hand tightened on my hip as we strode into my idea of a nightmare. There were hundreds of people on the dance floor in front of us, packed in elbow-to-elbow. Energy seemed to radiate from them, or maybe just from the deafeningly-loud music.

Crimson smoke billowed off them en masse, and my eyes widened at the sight of it.

Lust.

So much lust.

No wonder the guys came to nightclubs to feed.

Off to our left, there was a bar with half a dozen bartenders working. Almost every stool around it was full.

To our right, there were two rows of tables. The lights around them were dim, and my eyes went wider when I saw the lust rising from that part of the club.

Hot damn.

Raf tucked something in my ear, and I jerked toward him. He tapped his own ear, and the soft silk of his voice murmured directly into mine,

“So we can hear each other.”

“Bash and I are heading out. You’ll have company soon, I’m sure. Watch your backs.” Zander’s voice followed Rafael’s.

Since all of the guys were connected over our comms, I went up on my tiptoes and called to Raf, “What do we do?”

The music was so loud, I nearly had to yell.

He gave me a half-smile, then pulled me toward the dancing crowd.

I nearly shuddered at the idea of being sucked into the crowd and trapped between all those moving bodies.

He noticed my reaction and changed gears, turning and leading me toward the booths.

Where the lust was even thicker.

I was worried it would affect me somehow, but at least it wasn’t the crowd of dancers.

And anyway, we were there to get Miles back. I would deal with whatever I had to.

I tried not to look at the people inside as we passed them, but it was difficult. The booths were cube-shaped, so they were blocked off almost entirely from the rest of the club, but the openings faced us. My face reddened when I saw a few ass cheeks in one, and in the process of turning my head, I saw some random lady's bare boobs, and realized a guy had his fangs buried in her neck.

Yikes.

I stepped closer to Rafael.

He held me to his side before he stopped in front of a booth that had been roped off by whoever owned the nightclub. Eric Reiner, most likely.

Raf moved the divider, then tucked me into the booth before him. The music grew a little muffled thanks to the walls around us, and I relaxed into the cushions for a moment.

"Northern hallway is clear. Eight vamps down," Zander said into my ear.

Bash's voice followed. "Southern clear too. Four down on my side."

My eyes widened.

"Unconscious," Raf said. "We only kill when we're positive they deserve it."

I relaxed slightly.

His lips curved upward as he slid over to me, wrapping his arm around my back again. "Not a fan of nightclubs?"

I made a face, and he chuckled, pulling me closer. "I saw a vampire in one of those booths."

"Vampires own and run most of the nightclubs around the world," he agreed. "They can't feed at a distance like us, so it benefits them to have a place where they can find food easily. Most men and women who frequent clubs have been propositioned by a vamp at one point or another."

"Wow."

"You'll get to know the supernatural side of the world more, the longer you're in it." He kissed my shoulder. "Eric will join us any time. Let me do the talking, please. I don't want any more of his attention on you than you already have. The man is insane."

I nodded, and we sat back in the booth and waited.

twenty
TATUM

WE DIDN'T HAVE to wait long.

A tall man with pale skin and white-blond hair slipped into the booth with us, sandwiched on either side by what I assumed were his bodyguards.

"Give the girl back, Eric." Rafael didn't waste time beating around the bush, or even attempt to charm the bastard. "Her best friend has a hoard of dragon shifters for brothers; do you really want to bring them into this?"

Something flickered in Eric's eyes.

It looked a hell of a lot like fear.

It was gone as soon as it had appeared, of course.

Bash and Zander noted a few more rooms were clear, but I barely heard them.

Reiner drawled, "What is there to get into? All I have to do is put the property in your name and report the death, and the government will believe you've killed her. I'll have the pleasure of knowing that you get to watch your pretty little mate starve in prison."

Rafael's arm tightened around my waist just slightly, but he chuckled. "If it were that easy, I'd already be back behind bars. You're desperate; desperation makes you sloppy."

"You would know, wouldn't you? After stumbling into that coffee shop and talking a human into accepting you as her mate."

I didn't let my gaze jerk toward Rafael's.

How did Eric know that?

Raf's lips curved upward. "If lying to yourself about my mate makes you feel better, go ahead. We both know you're pissed that I managed to keep her from you until we sealed the bond. It would've been much easier to kill her while I was locked away, wouldn't it?"

Eric's eyes slitted, his smirk still pasted on his face. "I've never killed a human. Never would, either."

"Of course not. Unlike your sister, you're far too civil for that."

Eric shot to his feet, slamming his palms on the table as he leaned over it. Rafael squeezed my hip just before he did, so I didn't jump at the vampire's sudden outburst.

For the first time, I saw the gleam of madness in the man's eyes. "She only killed the humans who deserved it."

"You sincerely believe that *hundreds* of humans deserved to die as painfully as she killed them over the centuries?" Rafael's voice was still smooth.

He was keeping the vampire occupied while his brothers worked through the building.

Their voices were still in our ears every minute or two, as they moved through it.

"Humans are cattle. Their deaths don't weigh on my conscience any more than they weighed on hers." Eric sat back down. "Now, we're here for a trade. Your mate, for her friend."

"We both know that's not going to happen." Rafael's fingers dug into my hip, despite his words. "You're going to give us the girl, or you're going to be our next target."

Eric laughed darkly. "As if you don't have demons filtered through the nightclub already while your brothers search the rooms. I may be old, but I'm not stupid. She's not here."

My stomach clenched.

We really had gone in blind.

"I have no idea what you're talking about." Rafael lied easily.

Too easily.

"I don't—"

Eric cut himself off when a thick, tattooed body stepped into the booth's entrance. August slid in, sitting down next to Rafael, and all four of the men with me looked equally surprised to see him. Raf hid it better than the rest of them, but I could see through his mask.

"What the fuck is going on here?" August glared around the table.

There was a moment of silence as none of the guys answered.

Or as all of them tried to come up with a decent answer.

But I didn't look at them; I was too busy staring at August.

There was *so much* of Brynn in his face. In his scowl. In the color of his eyes, and the shape of his nose. They were definitely siblings.

I might not have officially met her brothers, but I had heard dozens of stories about them. They had basically raised her, they always came into town and took her out to eat for her birthday, they ordered an assload of candy from her shop that she didn't know if they even ate...

Despite the obvious differences between humans and shifters, I didn't believe that any of Brynn's brothers wouldn't care that her best friend had been taken and turned against her will.

So, I broke my promise to Raf and told him the truth. My hand swept toward Eric. "This guy paid someone to seduce Miley, then abducted her and turned her to a vampire. Now, she's starving to death. We're trying to save her life, but the only trade he'll accept is my life for Miles'."

August blinked at me.

Eric blinked at me.

Rafael blinked at me, too.

"Do you have proof?" the dragon finally asked.

I looked at Rafael, who slipped his phone out of his pocket. He pulled up the video of Miles, and I forced myself to look away when he slid it over to August. It wouldn't do me any good to tear up while surrounded by five massive supernaturals.

August's eyes narrowed as the video played. When it ended, he slid it back to Rafael, lifting his glare to Eric.

"If it's on his phone, it's evidence that he has the girl," Eric attempted to counter. "I'm the one here to argue for the girl's rescue."

"Miley's been under the Villins' protection since Rafael and I mated. Brynn has too. Call her; you know she'll tell you the truth," I said quickly.

August silently pulled his phone from his pocket and tapped a few buttons. Another minute or two passed, and then he lifted the phone to his ear.

"Where are you?"

Brynn's voice was muffled. "It's a long story, but shit went down. The Villins are keeping me safe right now. Why?"

He didn't answer her question. "Where's Miley?"

There was a long pause.

When she spoke, her voice was too quiet for me to hear the answer.

"I'll take care of it." The grit in August's voice was enough to scare the shit out of me.

Bash and Zander's voices filled our ears. "She's not here. The place is empty. We're headed back to meet you and deal with Reiner."

If I hadn't already been plastered to Rafael's side, I would've scooted closer.

August hung up, slipped his phone into his pocket, and then set his hands on the table.

Eric's face paled as the dragon shifter slowly lifted his gaze back to the vampire's.

August said, his voice low and gritty, "Get the girl's location into the Villins' hands in the next two minutes, or I'll drag you and your entire fucking clan to the prison. While you all starve to death, I'll make sure all of them know they're there because of *you.*"

The fear in Eric's eyes was so thick, I could almost taste it. He jerked his head in a nod, and typed something into his phone. A moment later, Rafael's phone buzzed.

He opened the message and found a link that went to a live camera. Miles was on the screen, fighting against the chains on her wrists. The gray on her feet and ankles had spread up to the middle of her thighs since the last video, and fear made my heart pound hard. There were coordinates on the page too, and I assumed that was the location.

"Got it?" August asked Raf.

"Yes. Thank you." Rafael lifted his gaze to the dragon's.

August dipped his head. "As far as anyone's concerned, this conversation never happened."

"Agreed."

"I'm going to walk away now. If the vampire leaves this table alive, I will carry *you* back to prison. Are we clear?"

"Crystal." Rafael's gaze moved back to the vampires', whose eyes were narrowing. "Escort my mate to the door."

I opened my mouth to protest—and then realized that was stupid, because I couldn't fight a damn vampire.

So I closed it.

And when Rafael lifted me over his lap and August grabbed my arm, I let him lead me away from the table. The man basically had to drag me along, because my attention was on the booth behind me.

All hell broke loose the moment I was gone. I heard a table crash into something—or someone—and terror cut through me.

My gaze caught on Bash and Zander, and I gestured frantically toward the booth. Tapping the device in my ear, I said, "Raf's in there with Eric and his bodyguards."

The brothers sprinted for the booth. Before they reached it, Rafael stepped out.

His hands were covered in blood, the tattoos, wings, and horns of his demon form vanishing as quickly as they had appeared.

He nodded at his brothers, and they slowed.

August let go of my arm and kept walking, calling over his shoulder, "Have the Villins send me my sister's location."

I sure as hell wasn't going to argue with him.

Raf grabbed my arm and pulled me in close to his side as we headed for the door. His hands were bloody, but neither of us cared.

"Our guys will clean up the mess," Zander told me, when he noticed me peeking over my shoulder. "There won't be evidence left to find."

Good.

That was good.

And now, it was time to get Miley back.

twenty-one

RAFAEL

I HELD Tatum to my chest as Bash hauled ass to the warehouse Miles was being held at. When I told her we were staying in the car while they got Miley out, she didn't argue.

She did ask why, though.

When I explained that Miles would be starving, and I didn't want her on the dinner plate, she grew quiet.

Her eyes watered a little, too.

But she didn't argue.

Twenty minutes later, Zander came out with Miley in his arms. She was shaking, but the gray on her legs had faded back to its proper color, and she had shifted out of her vampire form.

Zander set Miles in the passenger seat and buckled her in, then disappeared back into the building. She curled up in a ball against the door, and didn't say a word or look back at us.

Tatum flashed me an uncertain look, and I shook my head silently, telling her to give her friend space.

The fact that Miley wasn't attacking us meant she'd drained a hell of a lot of blood from *someone*. My bet was on Bash.

Sure enough, when Zander came out again, he was basically carrying Bash.

I left Tatum on the seat with a kiss, stepping out to help with my older brother.

"That tiny thing packs a punch," Bash mumbled, as we eased him to the car. "She's tougher than she looks."

For once, neither of us had a smartass response.

We eased him into the seat next to Tatum's, and Zander smacked him lightly on the thigh before walking around to the driver's seat.

Bash's quiet classical music floated through the car during the ride back. Tatum whispered that I needed to text the apartment's location to August, so I got his number from Brynn and did so.

Miles finally stopped shaking a few minutes before we got back, and fell into a fitful sleep.

"She'll need to eat again soon after she wakes up," Zander said, meeting Tatum's eyes in the mirror.

"Brynn and I will feed her," Tatum said, her jaw set.

"It'll be easier for her if she starts with bagged blood. Less overwhelming. I can head out and find some, if you're good with talking to her about it."

Relief relaxed her shoulders. "That would be great."

Zander nodded.

"I know a few vamps in the city who should have stashes. I'll make a few calls," I said.

I spent the last few minutes of the drive on the phone, and texted Zander a pair of addresses for vampires who had reluctantly offered some of their bagged blood.

He carried Miles, and I hauled Bash's heavy ass, with Tatum attempting to help me hold my brother's weight. My gaze moved over her face as we waited for the elevator, and I let out a long, quiet breath.

She was safe.

Reiner was dead.

If I looked at her from the side, like I was, I could almost convince myself that life was going to go back to how it had been since we'd moved in together.

Blissful.

Hot.

Fun.

It had been so long since I had as much pure *fun* as I had when I was with Tatum. The woman was sunshine, wrapped in a sarcastic, defensive, cinnamon-haired shell.

But I had hurt her.

And I had no idea how to fix that.

If she needed time, I'd give her time, but I wasn't going to make it easy for her to leave me.

She would be damn sure *I* wasn't walking away.

twenty-two

TATUM

"EASY," I murmured to Miley, when she sat up quickly. Her usually-gray eyes were a faded shade of red, and she clutched the blanket we'd draped over her like it was a lifeline.

Blinking, her head jerked as she looked around the apartment.

And slowly, her body relaxed a little.

We'd thought it was best for her to wake up in mine and Raf's apartment, since she had been there a handful of times before.

"What happened?" Her voice was raspy, like her throat was dry. "Where's Brynn?"

"She's in the apartment next door, talking to her brother. Apparently, Raf, Bash, and Zander own this apartment complex." I rolled my eyes at her. I'd been instructed to act as normal as possible to make sure she knew I didn't see her differently, so I was doing my best.

Miles didn't seem to hear anything I had said, staring down at her hands. They didn't look any different to me, but maybe they did to her.

"What happened, Tatum?" Her voice was quieter, the second time. More desperate.

If I was treating her normally, I couldn't beat around the bush. We didn't do that with each other.

"Evan was working with some vampires who wanted revenge on the Villins. I don't know what happened when they abducted you, but they turned you, and then starved you. We got to you as fast as we could, and you drank a lot of Bash's blood. He's fine, and he was glad to help out. The big bastard had too much blood anyway."

My joke didn't hit; she didn't smile.

It really wasn't that funny, but I tried anyway.

"The memories are fuzzy, but here." Her eyes closed for a long moment. "I'm still hungry. You smell good. Not like family—like a meal. How messed up is that?"

"It's normal, Miles. You can drink from me, if you want. But Zander will be back any time now with bagged blood, if you'd prefer to eat that way."

"That might be easier." She leaned back against the couch, pulling her knees to her chest.

The door swung open, and Zander stepped inside. There was a massive ice chest in his arms, but he stopped just inside the door.

Lust immediately broke out over his arms and shoulders, and I followed his gaze to Miley.

There was a little lust coming off her, too, which was unusual for her.

"He smells *really* good," Miles whispered, quiet enough that Zander couldn't have heard her. Her eyes were glued to him.

When I looked back, he was still staring at her.

Anastasia's explanation about a guy who'd found a potential mate echoed in my ears, but I couldn't say it aloud. Miles had never wanted a life partner. If Zander did, he would've already tracked one down.

"I'm, uh..." He trailed off.

Miley finally shook her head, snapping out of it.

Zander abruptly dropped the ice chest by the door. "I've gotta go. Blood's in there. Good luck."

With that, he disappeared out the door.

I blinked.

Miley started to get up, but I patted her leg lightly. "I'll grab it. The guys said you need to rest."

She nodded, her face a little red as she relaxed back against the couch cushions. "Sorry. Thank you."

"If one of us should be apologizing, it's me. I'm the bitch who brought you into all of this." I crossed the room and dragged the ice chest into the kitchen. "Cold, warm, or hot?"

She grimaced. "Hot. And it's not your fault—I'm the moron who thought a vampire might actually be interested in me."

I made a face. "I did the same with a demon, so I can't blame you."

"Rafael is *not* like Evan." She peeled a tangled, sweat-crusted chunk of curls off the side of her face, tucking it behind her ear. "He loves you. Anyone with eyes can see that. He even sent his brothers in to rescue and feed me. I think I knocked the poor guy unconscious."

"You did, but only for a minute." I put a few bags of blood under hot, running water, and then started moving everything else in the ice chest to the freezer. "Bash won't hold it against you."

"I hope not." She closed her eyes again, letting out a long, shaky breath. "What do I do now? Where do I go from here?"

"You don't *go* from here. Raf and his brothers really do own the apartment complex; Rafael will move out. You'll stay here, with me and Brynn. B and I can snuggle."

Her expression grew grave. "What if I hurt you guys?"

"I'm a demon. Pretty sure it takes more than a little blood-sucking to kill me."

"Brynn isn't."

"Then she can stay next door."

Miley sighed. "I don't know, Tatum."

"You don't have to know. We'll figure it out as we go, like we did with the first shop."

She gave me a tiny smile. "I need to check on my manager."

"Brynn already called her. Your shop is doing fine."

"That's good, I guess."

"You guess?" I teased lightly.

Her tiny smile returned, but faded quickly. "I need a plan. I just wasn't expecting any of this. I'll figure it out."

"Of course you will."

Her gaze moved to the massive windows, and lingered on the view. "This really is a beautiful apartment. Can't beat the view."

"It is," I agreed.

Her voice was soft. "You should stay with him. You're happy with him. I can move to one of their other apartments, if this is really the safest place."

The hurt and anger I'd buried to deal with the shitty situation surfaced, and my throat swelled. "I can't. He lied to me."

"About what?"

"He never told me we were in danger. I didn't know he had people following you guys, to keep you safe. I didn't know I needed to worry."

"Those aren't lies, Tatum. A lie hurts someone. Rafael didn't tell you everything, but he didn't hurt you—the situation did. Brynn and I knew his guys were following us. They weren't sneaky about it. I slipped away from them to meet Evan without being watched, because he told me he wanted privacy. My stupid decisions were my fault, and no one else's."

"He still should've told me. I trusted that he would tell me if I was in danger or if you guys were. I can't just let that go." I finished transferring everything in the ice chest to the freezer, then opened the door and dragged the chest outside.

When the door was shut again, Miley said, "I get it. I just want more for you. He's a good guy, and he loves you."

"If he does, he's never told me." I checked the blood bags, finding them mostly thawed. "Do you think you can microwave blood?"

Miles snorted. "Of all the questions we never thought we'd have to ask."

I smiled. "I'll ask Zander."

Almost as soon as I'd sent the message, he answered an affirmative with instructions. He added that when he picked it up, he'd been given warning not to heat it too long, or she wouldn't be able to choke it down.

"Do you want to drink it in a bag or a cup?" I asked.

"I don't deserve a cup at this point. Bring the bag over."

"For that, you get a cup." I opened the cupboard with a flourish and pulled out one of Rafael's undoubtedly-expensive glasses. "A *fancy* one."

It earned me another small smile. "You've been happier, since you moved in with him. Don't let him go so easily."

The door opened, and Brynn slipped inside while Miles finished talking. Her eyes brightened when she saw Miley awake and upright, but she didn't make a big deal about it. "Don't let who go so easily?"

"Rafael. She wants to drop him."

"I can't *drop* him. We're mated permanently. He'd probably punch any other guy I tried to date. I want space from him, so I can decide whether or not I can still trust him at all after he kept so many things from me," I corrected.

"Space can be good." Brynn headed toward the couch, and Miley pointed at her.

"Stay there."

Brynn halted, and blinked.

"Your cute human self smells too good to her," I explained for Miles, who grimaced but nodded.

Brynn backed up before plopping down on one of the barstools. "How's this?"

"Better." Miley relaxed a little. "And space is fine, as long as Rafael knows you're not trying to leave him permanently."

"Rafael isn't going to *let* her leave him permanently. He's her mate," Brynn said, matter-of-factly. "We should make bets on how long he gives her before he drags her ass back into his life."

Miles' lips curved upward. "What should we bet on?"

"You are *not* betting on me getting back with a guy who didn't tell me the truth about being in danger," I shot back, pulling the first bag of blood from the microwave. "If I'd known, I would've been more suspicious of Evan. I would've warned you."

"And I wouldn't have listened," Miley said matter-of-factly.

"She is pretty stubborn," Brynn pointed out.

"We're all pretty stubborn, but we still take each other's advice."

"I thought I was in love with him." She turned back to the windows, her gaze lingering on the mountains again. "After a few *days*. How messed up is that? I'm never having sex again. It messed with my mind too damn much."

"August just claimed my spare bed, so we can be sad and lonely together with all those cats and dogs," Brynn offered.

I snorted.

Miles grimaced. "Yay."

I finished filling up a second cup with blood, and brought both of them over to her. Her grimace deepened when she accepted them, but her eyes closed. Her nails grew sharper, and I saw the faint outline of tattoos appearing on her skin as she gripped the glasses.

The guys had made it sound like drinking blood would be a hard adjustment for her, and I knew Miles preferred to cope in private. So, I grabbed Brynn's arm and tugged her off the barstool.

"We'll give you a few minutes. I thawed a couple more bags and texted you the instructions on how to warm them up, in case you're still hungry," I said.

"Good luck!" Brynn called out.

RAFAEL, August, and Bash were all sitting at the table when we walked into the other apartment. Raf had just showered, so his hair was wet and he was dressed in clean, casual clothes. Bash looked slightly disheveled for the first time since I'd met him. And August... well, he looked normal. For him, normal seemed to be ripped jeans and a tight t-shirt.

The men were deep in conversation about how they tracked and killed murderous vampires, but Rafael abandoned his seat the moment we stepped inside the room. He pulled me into his arms, and mine wrapped around him automatically.

Brynn slipped past us with a quick smile, taking the seat Rafael had been sitting in without stopping to ask permission. August was between her and Bash, but Bash's body stiffened as he continued explaining.

"How is she?" Rafael's voice was low, smooth, and still gave me the damn goosebumps.

My traitorous body didn't seem to get the memo that we were supposed to be mad at him.

"Dealing with it. She seems... lost."

"Her whole life just changed. Lost is reasonable." His hand moved slowly over my back.

"It is." I glanced at the group sitting at the table. They were focused, but I wasn't about to have a conversation about the future of our relationship with so many people around. "I need to shower; I still feel like there's blood on my skin. Let's talk in a few hours."

Raf dipped his head, brushing a kiss to my cheek before he strode back to the table and took the chair next to Bash's.

Letting out a long breath, I went up and took my second shower of the day.

BRYNN and I hung out in her new apartment until Miley texted us two hours later.

MILES

You can come back if you want.

We exchanged looks, and headed over immediately

Both of us stopped just inside the doorway when we found her sitting in the corner of the couch, snuggled up under multiple blankets. Her dark curls were loose and damp, and I could smell my shampoo from where we stood.

A glance at the kitchen showed everything was clean, and the smell of lemony disinfectant told me she had gone so far as to wipe down the countertops too.

The TV was on and a streaming service was open, but nothing was playing yet.

Miley peeked up from her blankets to look at us. "Can you make the popcorn with chocolate on it?"

I smiled. "Sure."

"Do I still smell delicious?" Brynn shimmied, and Miley's face softened.

"Not as much. Come snuggle."

Brynn crossed the room, vaulting over the back of the couch and plopping down next to Miley. She earned a snort, and my smile widened.

She was asking us for things, which was rare for Miles. It took a lot for her to ask for help, even in the form of popcorn and snuggling. We would be there for her, though, no matter what.

"What are we watching?" Brynn asked, cuddling up under the mountain of blankets.

"I don't know. Something without vampires, or blood."

"A cheesy Christmas movie it is," Brynn declared, grabbing the remote and pulling up a movie. "Too bad we don't have any of Tatum's peppermint truffles. I'd kill for one right now."

"We're not talking about killing, either," Miley said quickly.

"I'd cry for one," Brynn corrected.

"No need to cry. Rafael has his own stock of candy in here." I opened the fridge, pulling out the box still sitting where he'd left it. The sight of it made my throat swell.

I brought the box over to the couch while the popcorn popped, then whipped up the toppings and drizzled them over it, one by one. Without waiting for it to cool, I brought a bowl of the messy treat to the couch.

"Now, I can die happy," Miley mumbled around a mouthful of popcorn.

"We're not talking about death," Brynn reminded her, through her own mouthful.

I tucked my legs under the blankets with the girls', content not to move for the rest of the day. I knew I'd need to have a conversation with Rafael, but it could wait. "A human, demon, and vampire walked into a bar..."

Miley snorted, and Brynn laughed.

We started the movie, and it felt almost like the old times, when we were all broke and struggling to get our business started.

Almost like the old times...

But better.

Despite everything that had happened, I knew that if I could go back to the day Rafael stumbled into my coffee shop, I would do everything exactly the same way I already had.

And that scared the shit out of me.

twenty-three

TATUM

I FELL asleep on the couch without talking to Rafael. I woke up a little when I heard him come in to check on me, and I felt him brush my hair off my face before he murmured that we would talk in the morning. He left me where I was with a soft kiss to my cheek that earned a sleepy smile as I closed my eyes again.

The next morning, Miley seemed distant as Brynn made the three of us breakfast. There were a few texts on my phone from Zander that said he'd been doing research about vampires, and had learned that new vamps needed a lot of blood while they were transitioning. Apparently, he had picked up the ice chest and would drop off more blood that day.

I didn't let myself overthink the situation, or consider what I was suspicious about.

If Miles or Zander wanted a mate, they would figure it out themselves. Me getting involved was a bad idea, especially considering it could wreck the peace between my friend group and the Villin brothers.

Brynn was tired of being cooped up, so she headed to her shop with August on her tail—and the Villins' security detail on *his* tail, if I had to guess.

Miles put together a list of all the candy we needed to restock for each of the shops and finish to make our upcoming orders. The damn thing was a doozy. I had a lot of hours in the kitchen ahead of me.

But, a glance at Miley told me I wouldn't be cooking in Rafael's kitchen.

She was staring out at the mountains, holding a blanket to her chest.

She needed space, and time to process.

So, it was time to make myself scarce.

I sent her screenshots of Zander's texts so she knew everything he'd told me. Then I changed my clothes, hugged her, and grabbed the lanyard that held my keys, before heading out.

As soon as I stepped into the short hallway between our doors and the elevator, I halted.

Rafael was leaned up against the wall, his hands tucked in the pockets of his joggers. His hair was a mess and his t-shirt was rumpled, but his lips still curved upward when he saw me. "Hey, Tater-tot."

Shit, my heart actually skipped a beat. "Hey, Riffraff."

His lips curved further.

I couldn't let myself get caught up in him again, though. Not until I figured out what I really wanted, and if I could trust him again.

I hit the button for the elevator, and when the doors opened, Rafael slipped into it beside me.

He didn't touch me, and I didn't touch him.

The distance was foreign. Really damn foreign.

Then again, what wasn't foreign between us? We were back in the apartment we'd shared, but it felt like *his*. He had kept secrets from me, which made me feel like he didn't see us as equals. We still couldn't be apart physically, but now, it felt like there was a huge wall separating us emotionally.

Where did we go from there?

"I have to spend all day making candy at the coffee shop," I said, my voice quiet and a little uncertain.

"Our kitchen won't work?"

"Miles processes better on her own. If we smother her, she won't come to us when she really needs us. She's comfortable in your apartment, so I don't want to ask her to leave. Is there somewhere else you can stay?" I didn't meet his gaze, knowing that whatever I saw on his face would change how I felt.

"Just me?" His voice was careful.

"She needs me to stay with her right now, and I need space to decide what I want to do about us," I admitted.

"We're mates, Tatum. The only thing to *do* is figure out how to get past this. Even if I could, I wouldn't let you go."

His hand landed on my arm, and he carefully turned me toward him, tilting my head back until our eyes met.

The elevator's doors opened, but neither of us moved to get off.

"You hurt me," I said quietly. "You kept things from me, and it hurt me. If we're going to move on, you have to give me time to decide I'm ready for that."

His Adam's apple bobbed.

His forehead lowered to mine, and rested against it. My eyes fluttered closed, and his thumb dragged slowly over my cheek.

I hadn't realized how much I missed touching him until that moment.

"I'll give you a week," he finally murmured, his lips nearly brushing mine as he spoke.

My face twisted in a scowl, and he kissed me lightly before he let me pull away from him. "You don't get to decide when I forgive you, Raf."

His lips curved upward slightly. "You can be mad at me as long as you want, Tater-tot—I meant I give it a week before you miss me too much to keep hating me."

My scowl deepened, and I turned on my heel. When I realized the elevator's doors had shut, I halted.

Rafael pushed a button, and they opened again with a ding.

He followed me into the parking garage, to the row I was pretty sure I had parked my car in the last time we'd driven it. It had been a while, but I was pretty sure it should be there...

Frowning, I hit the lock button to make it beep.

The sound was different, and came from the other side of the garage.

I hit it again when I was over there, and my eyes narrowed when I realized what had happened.

Marching up to the back of *a* car, I spun to face Raf. "Where did you put my car?"

"This *is* your car. A safer, upgraded version of it. One our enemies can't track, or hack. We replaced your friends' as well."

I didn't want to let him win...

But after what had happened with Miley, I could see the necessity.

Letting out a huff, I unlocked the doors and dropped into the driver's seat.

Rafael had even moved that up for me, so I didn't have to spend five minutes waiting for the damn thing to move into place given our height difference. He was too damn thoughtful.

"You could've *told* me," I said as he let himself in on the passenger side, taking the seat without asking.

"I did. Bash and I were texting about it in the group chat, which you're a part of."

My fingers tightened on the steering wheel.

Shit.

I had seen notifications on the group chat that morning, but hadn't gotten around to reading the messages.

His voice was gentle as he said, "I know you think I'm the bad guy here, Tater-tot, but I swear it's never been my intention to hurt you. I've done my damndest to protect people for most of my life; I've been trying to protect you too, in the only ways I know how. I should have told you about the danger, and next time, I will without hesitation."

He was right.

I *knew* he was right, and that made it worse, somehow.

Harder, too.

He had hurt me, but it wasn't an intentional attack. Since I told him there could be no secrets between us, he had seemed to be trying for transparency.

"I know you're a good man, Raf. You're not a murderer; you're a hero. I've never been under the impression that you would tell me *everything*, but I trusted that you would tell me the important things. I don't know how to get that trust back." I finally pulled out of the parking space, forced to admit silently that the car was absolutely a dream.

He hadn't picked the most expensive car at the dealership; he'd bought the one he knew I would choose for myself.

"I obviously haven't been open enough, if you feel that way," he said, watching the road while I merged into traffic. "I'll become an obnoxiously-open book."

"I'll believe that when I see it."

He chuckled. "Tell me the things you want to know more about."

"The apartment building. How much of it do you own?"

"I just have the one floor, with four apartments on it. To reach the other two apartments, you have to take the building's other elevators. It's harder to function as an unmated demon when there are people around constantly, so I needed the space. Zander has a floor too, a few above mine. Bash owns the rest of it. He has renters in most of the building."

That made me feel a little better. I wasn't as clueless as I thought.

"Bash doesn't live in the complex," Rafael added. "He has a house in the mountains that he prefers, and another on the outskirts of the city for when he needs to be close. He likes to stay far enough away that he doesn't have to deal with people. Zander usually doesn't live there either; he has a house in the busiest part of the downtown. The bastard likes to be in the middle of the commotion, even though he doesn't usually get involved."

My shoulders relaxed a little more. "How many houses do you own?" He had told me he didn't have any in the city—or had at least offered to buy me one, when we first got mated. I hadn't brought it up again, but I still wanted to know.

"Around the world? A dozen. I don't have one in this city. I've never cared much about business, so I've never focused on stockpiling wealth and collecting houses."

That made me feel even better.

"You are rich, though?"

"We've established that, Tater-tot. It's easy enough to invest in safe, long-term shit and turn a profit when you have the funds and the time."

I supposed that made sense. "I want you to take me to the bank today, to prove it. I don't want to be worried that you're lying to me or keeping things from me anymore."

"Turn here." He gestured to a street, and I turned a little faster than I probably should've. He laughed when the tires squealed, and I grinned sheepishly.

"Not used to the new car yet."

"If that's what you have to tell yourself."

A laugh escaped me, and I smacked him on the leg. He caught my hand, lifting it to his lips and pressing a kiss to the back before he released it.

After a few more directions, I was parked in front of a bank.

I left the car running for a minute, rather than rushing out. He walked around to my side and opened my door for me, offering me a hand.

I looked up at him instead. "I'm being insecure, aren't I?"

"Nah. Even if you were, a little insecurity won't kill either of us. If proving this to you makes you feel even the tiniest bit better, I'm happy to do it." He leaned over to unbuckle me, then stepped back and took my hand. When he towed me out, I couldn't stop myself from slipping my fingers between his.

Damn traitorous body.

WE SPENT three hours across five different banks in town. Rafael pulled the information from a sixth up on his phone when we left the last one, followed by an online folder of deeds, titles, and pictures of the houses and vehicles he owned around the world.

Everything that Raf owned was already mine too.

My name was already on every one of them.

It was quite the mindfuck, seeing it next to Rafael's.

Tatum Villin.

"I *know* you didn't mention me taking your last name," I finally said, as I handed back his phone. My mind was spinning, but not in a bad way.

Not even a little.

He flashed me a roguish grin and pulled out of the parking lot. He'd taken my place in the driver's seat a few banks earlier, and I hadn't had any desire to take it back. "Supernaturals are old-fashioned. The change was automatic. I put your new license in your wallet a few weeks ago; you just haven't noticed."

I pulled the wallet out, and sure enough, it was the same hideous picture on a completely different ID.

Under *Tatum Villin*, there was a section that said *Supernatural Type: Demon.*

I stared at it for a while.

A little too long, honestly.

As I put the license away, I noticed that my wallet was thicker than usual.

Much thicker than usual.

I opened the cash section, and my head immediately jerked toward Rafael. "Why the hell do I have so much cash?"

"I had to pay you for the candy I stole, remember?"

I wiggled the bills out and flipped through them. "We agreed on three hundred, Raf. You spent way more than that on food alone while we were living together. And this is three *thousand* dollars. How long have I been walking around with this much money?!"

As far as I could remember, I hadn't gotten my wallet out since...

Well, since Rafael showed up in the coffee shop.

We were almost constantly together, and he had paid for *everything*. The fitness classes I'd taken with Miles and Brynn were online payments, and when they hadn't gone through, I'd checked online and even found his card attached to my account.

After seeing how much money he had, I didn't feel even the tiniest bit bad for letting him pay, but still.

It was the principle of the matter.

"I put it in there a few days after we mated."

I sighed, leaning back against my chair. "You're making it really hard to stay mad at you. Apparently, I can be seduced with money and joggers."

"You should've told me how much you hated my suits earlier," he said, shaking his head. "If I'd known joggers were the way to seduce you, you'd be putty in my hands by now."

I snorted. "It seemed like a part of my life that didn't have to affect you. It wasn't anything against you—you just didn't have to know."

As I said the words, I understood Rafael's point of view little more.

Wasn't he in the same position?

I didn't like his clothes, and as far as he'd known, I didn't like his job. We both kept our thoughts to ourselves because it seemed easier. Obviously, his silence had more of an impact than mine, but the concept was the same.

"Well, like I said, I'm entirely invested in making myself as attractive to you as possible. Next time, tell me." His hand landed on my thigh for the first time all day, and he squeezed lightly.

"I will." The words were honest.

He squeezed my thigh one more time, then released it.

And I found myself wondering how long I'd really be able to keep up the distance I put between us.

twenty-four

TATUM

RAFAEL HELPED me in the kitchen until Sophie closed up for the day. He got along with her and the rest of my employees so well, it was ridiculous. It was good to catch up with everyone, but I was honestly relieved when Sophie locked up and slipped out.

When she was gone, I shooed him out of the kitchen while I turned on my music so I could jam out and work alone. He sprawled out in one of the booths with his phone, and I couldn't stop my gaze from going to him every time I walked that way.

When I was finally done, I made him a cup of coffee and shut off the music. After padding over to him, I plopped down on the bench next to him. He immediately pulled me onto his lap, and I peered down at his phone screen. "Is that a *house*?"

"Mmhm. My landlady evicted me a few hours ago."

I was the landlady.

And I guess I kind of *had* evicted him.

Whoops.

"She sounds like a bitch," I said, plucking the phone from his hand and looking through the pictures.

"She had a good reason." He kissed my neck lightly. "But my mate has always wanted to buy a house anyway, so it's the perfect opportunity."

"Well, *she* sounds high maintenance."

"No. She's perfect the way she is."

"This place is gorgeous, Raf." I looked up from the phone, leaning to the side so I could meet his eyes. It wasn't the ridiculous mansion I would've expected when we met, just a spacious house with every possible upgrade. Oh, and a kitchen big enough to make me shed a tear or three. "Did you buy it?"

"I know better than to pick out a house for us myself, Tater-tot. I texted you links for a dozen that I would be happy with; look through and pick your favorites. We'll go walk through them tomorrow." He brushed a loose strand of hair from my eyes.

"I'm supposed to be mad at you," I reminded him, though I hadn't really felt that since our conversation earlier.

"I support your anger. Ready to head home?"

There was no way to hold back my smile at his words. "I guess."

He drove us back to the complex, and I spent the whole drive looking at houses.

Gushing about them.

Critiquing them.

Going back and forth on which one I liked the most.

When I kissed him at the door to his old apartment, Rafael's smile told me he knew he had already won. I'd hold out a little longer, but forgiveness was inevitable.

BASH and a few of the guys they trusted had moved all of mine and Rafael's stuff out while I was gone, except a bag Miley packed for me while they were there. When they returned, they had all of Miles' stuff with them.

She spent the day organizing her things, and seemed more at-peace with the changes than I expected.

Brynn, Miles, and I all dug out our laptops as we settled on the couch for another Christmas movie. It was already late, and I still wasn't anywhere near caught up with the candy, but that was tomorrow's problem.

Because we were spending the night looking at houses.

We oohed and ahhed together, gushing and debating. As always, Brynn was the romantic one who fell in love with the elegant arches or floor-to-ceiling windows. And, as expected, Miley pointed out the potential positives and negatives of every option.

All of the houses were beautiful, though.

We couldn't decide.

That night, I curled up in mine and Raf's old bed with Brynn. The sheets and comforter were different than when we shared it, and everything smelled like laundry detergent.

Brynn sprawled out over almost the entire massive bed, but I didn't fall asleep right away.

Laying on my side, I stared at my phone for a solid five minutes before I finally picked it up and texted Rafael.

ME

Where are you sleeping?

RAF

On the couch in Brynn's new place. August isn't feeling generous with her bed, and he's got the spare

ME

I'm sorry

RAF

Don't be. I was an ass, so I deserve the punishment

He really hadn't been an ass, but I appreciated the sentiment anyway.

ME

How long do you think I have until my eyes go red?

RAF

Hard to say. It's different for everyone. My mom can go about a week, and then it hits her, and she's a damn menace until she eats. I've only seen it happen twice, when she and my dad disagreed about something.

ME

I can't imagine them fighting.

RAF

Both times, he had helped us gather evidence against a particularly powerful vamp. She was worried about him. No one blamed her for starving him for a few days, including him.

I couldn't stop the small smile that crept onto my face.

ME

I looked at the houses some more with Brynn and Miles. Still have no idea which ones I want to go see.

RAF

We'll tour all of them, then.

ME

That seems excessive

RAF

Welcome to demonhood ;)

My smile grew a little.

ME

I'm too behind on work to do it tomorrow. Everything's flying off the shelf, and we have all kinds of holiday orders coming up. It's going to be hectic.

RAF

Hire someone else to cook with you, or teach Brynn or Miles how to do it.

I blinked.

RAF

You'll still make good money with someone else taking over that part of the job. Your recipes are what keeps the customers coming back, not the fact that you're making them yourself.

He wasn't wrong.

ME

I'll think about it.

RAF

We can get up early to walk through the houses tomorrow and stay late again, if you're up for it.

ME

Fine, you've convinced me.

RAF

Damn, you are a hard woman

I laughed softly.

ME

That better be a compliment

RAF

Always

We settled on a time, and he said he'd make the appointments. As I put my phone back down on the nightstand, I was forced to admit a bitter, bitter truth.

I missed sleeping next to Rafael.

TOURING the houses the next morning was surreal. I knew I wanted the second one the moment we walked into it, but had to make sure before I committed.

After we saw the last one with the realtor, Raf told him to make an offer on the one I'd loved the most.

Then, we were back in the coffee shop, working on candy.

Christmas was only two weeks away, so the orders at the shop were growing larger and more frequent, which meant more time spent in the kitchen.

And the kitchen at *Coffee & Toffee* no longer felt adequate, after working in the spacious, quiet peace of mine and Raf's old apartment.

But, with the holiday around the corner, the house's seller had agreed to a quick closing. We'd get the keys as soon as they were done with the paperwork—which, according to Rafael, would be very soon.

The next few days passed quickly. I loved Miley and Brynn, but both of them seemed distant. Brynn was exhausted from being followed around by her brother all the time, and Miles was still trying to wrap her head around everything.

We all laughed about every new bouquet of flowers Rafael left at our door, though, usually one in the morning and one at night. The apartment was flooded with red roses, and all of them had a funny handwritten note attached.

I miss watching you detangle your hair with that adorable little annoyed expression.

Your ass looks awesome through the wall between us.

I don't have anything on beneath my joggers right now ;)

You make me happy. And horny.

I miss watching movies with your legs sprawled over my lap, and your sarcastic commentary.

That freckle on your thigh is begging to be licked again.

I miss being strangled by your hair while we sleep.

My smile grew sadder—and my remaining distrust grew smaller—with each day we spent together and each silly note.

I WOKE up a week before Christmas with a massive to-do list, and an even bigger headache.

My stomach hurt.

My chest hurt.

My head felt like someone had driven a nail into it.

And holy hell, I was *angry*. I couldn't even say why, I just was.

I stumbled into the bathroom, and scowled at my appearance.

My eyes were red. Of course the damn things were red. I should've seen that coming.

My anger, though definitely still there, faded slightly.

I had been avoiding the truth for a week at that point, and there was no more running from it.

I could tell Miley needed space from both of us.

And Brynn was planning on moving back to the apartment next door as soon as I was out, so our issues were keeping her stuck living a hall away from all of her stuff.

So I had to move out when Rafael and I got the keys.

The problem was, moving out meant jumping all-in with Rafael.

The thought made me more nervous than I wanted to admit.

The last time we lived together, we'd done it because we had no choice. Because we needed to fool people into thinking our relationship wasn't at its beginning.

I had moved into an apartment that belonged to him. We had our own beds, even if we didn't sleep apart. We were together because we had to be.

All of that would change.

We would be living together because we wanted to. In *our* house. One we decided on together, even if he'd given me final say. One we paid for from a bank account that had both our names on it.

We would be sharing *our* bed, along with the rest of *our* furniture.

Our relationship was real.

Our mate bond was real.

Our *marriage* was real.

And as much as I tried to fight it, I was in love with my husband.

Miles and Brynn were my family, but Rafael had become that too.

I trusted him.

I had fun with him.

And I was so damn tired of the distance I'd put between us.

"You look like shit," Brynn mumbled, leaning up against the doorway and pushing tangled hair out of her eyes. "Are you finally going to go after Rafael?"

"I am." I didn't bother pulling a brush through my hair or changing my clothes. Over my shoulder, I called, "Stay out of the hallway until I come back in."

Brynn laughed, and I flipped her off as I left.

My lips stretched in a grin when she laughed louder.

The door closed behind me, and I knocked loudly on the one to Brynn's apartment, where August and Raf were sleeping.

When no one answered immediately, I knocked louder. I couldn't remember the code, so I couldn't just let myself in.

When there *still* wasn't an answer, I yelled, "Open the damn door, Raf!"

There was a moment of silence, and then it swung open.

My mate was in the doorway, towering above me with all that yummy tan skin. All he had on was a pair of joggers, and his hair was a mess.

Perfect.

He was perfect.

His lips stretched in a sleepy, sexy smile, and the lust around him grew thicker and redder. "Feeling a little hungry, Tater-tot?"

I tugged him into the hallway, and he stepped out, closing the door behind him. His back thudded against it a heartbeat after it shut, when I pushed him up against the wood, pulling his mouth to mine and kissing him.

Hard.

He cupped my chin, tilting my head back further with one hand while he yanked me closer with the other. His erection met my lower belly, and we kissed.

It was perfect.

But I wanted more.

I hooked a leg around his waist to lift myself higher, and he moved. A breath later, *my* back hit the door, and both my legs were around him.

"You're hot when you're hungry," he murmured against my lips.

"You're always hot. Gotta keep up somehow."

He growled at me, rocking his cock against my clit in a way that made my breath hitch. "No insulting yourself. You're fucking perfect. Say it."

"I'm fucking perfect."

"That's right." He rocked against me again, and I groaned.

"I need you."

"Tell me you've missed me, first."

"I've missed you so much it's ridiculous." I cried out when he moved, my body tense after so long without a release. The man had trained me to need him—and I had no desire to go back.

"Tell me you're done pretending to be mad at me, Tater-tot."

"I'm done. I'm not mad. I just want you."

He moved his body away from mine just enough to yank my shirt off, and tossed it to the ground. "Tell me you're going to move in with me the moment our keys are ready."

"I am. I already decided I am."

"I'm not waiting for these panties to come off," he growled, tugging the lace to the side and lining the head of his cock up with my opening. "I want you now, Tatum."

"Take me, then," I demanded.

He thrust into me in one smooth motion, and took in a deep inhale of my lust.

My back arched at the intensity of the pleasure, and cries escaped me as his cock swelled while he shifted, setting off my orgasm.

"Feed, Tater-tot. Now." His command while I lost control was enough to make my body act. I took in his lust, and felt my body change.

One of his hands captured my tail, and the other gripped one of my horns, dragging over the sensitive tip. "I want to hear you scream for me."

"You're getting there," I moaned. Rafael had complete control of my body, and he knew it.

He took in another deep breath of my lust, and his wings spread out behind him. They had to have knocked against the walls.

I wanted Raf just as lost to me as I was to him. My hands were on his shoulders, holding my body to his...

So I slid them backward and buried them in the soft, crimson feathers.

Rafael's roar nearly shook the ground as he pounded into me, gripping my tail and horn so damn tightly it hurt. The fierce pressure on those sensitive bits sent me over the edge, and I screamed as we climaxed together, hard and fast.

Both of us took deep inhales of each other's lust as we came down from the high, neither of us done.

"Grabbing my feathers is a low blow, Tater-tot." His voice was silky, the tone of it nearly making me shiver.

"You'll have to pay me back for it, because I'm not letting go."

I tightened my grip, rocking against his cock.

His eyes flashed, and his hands released my tail and horn, sliding over my wings.

It felt like he was touching my damn soul.

"We're never living apart again. If I piss you off, you fight with me about it until we've reached a solution that satisfies us both," he said.

"Agreed."

"You're mine, permanently. Say it." He thrust into me while he slowly dragged his hands over my wings, the pleasure so intense I felt like I was flying.

"I'm yours, forever."

"Now drink, gorgeous. I want my lust on your tongue when you shatter."

I did as he said—and we shattered together, again.

Our chests heaved as the pleasure faded, but our eyes were still locked together.

"I love you, Tater-tot. I've loved you since I was in prison, dreaming about you, and I'll love you long after we both leave this Earth. *Aeternum.*"

My eyes stung as I recognized the word. The one he'd spoken to me in the coffee shop, to seal our bond. "*Aeternum,* Raf. I love you too."

He captured my mouth in his, and made love to me again.

Slower.

Sweeter.

And with so damn much emotion, I wished it would never end.

RAFAEL

WE DID what Tatum called a "walk of shame" back into our old apartment. I didn't think it qualified, because I was shameless, but the red on her cheeks and the grins her friends shot her way made her certain it was shameful.

I'd texted her the night before to let her know we were getting the keys that morning, but the woman hadn't looked at her messages before coming over to grab me.

Or before *coming* all over my cock, repeatedly.

So we packed her bag, stopped to grab mine, and then headed out. Most of our things were already boxed, which made that easier.

"Can demons fly?" she asked me on the way to the house, curiosity in her voice. My hand was moving over the inside of her thigh, and she hadn't tried to stop me. Finally, we were done with the damn space between us.

"We can, but not far. Our wings are mostly for pleasure. I'll take you flying behind our house after we get everything set up. The movers are set to drop our furniture and boxes off while we work, and Bash and Zander are planning on being there to help haul everything into place as soon as we get back from the shop."

Her eyes brightened, the gorgeous green making my cock hard all over again.

I would never have enough of her.

"I talked to Brynn about taking over more baking after the holidays are over," Tatum said. "She was actually really excited; it gives her more space from August, now that he's staying with her. We're going to set up the schedule so she does two-thirds of the cooking, to factor in time for me to work on the recipes. And to travel with you, when we need to."

My gaze jerked to her, and I had to hit the brake harder than I preferred when the light turned red as I looked back at the road. "What?"

"You save humans' lives. I can't in good conscience ask you to stop protecting people, especially knowing how much you enjoy it. You support me with the bakery; it's time for me to support you in... well, murdering vampires."

I laughed. "Thanks, Tater-tot."

"You're welcome. I'm kind of looking forward to traveling, anyway. I haven't seen much of the world, and I'm going to make you show me the most beautiful places everywhere we go."

"Of course." I snagged her hand and lifted it to my lips, pressing a kiss to her knuckles. "I love you."

Her cheeks went my favorite shade of red. “I love you too.”

I pulled up to the bakery, parking in the same spot her old car had been the day I got out of prison.

I had spent a year in hell, but it brought me to the woman I loved.

...even if we’d taken an unconventional route to get there.

epilogue

TATUM—6 MONTHS LATER

"FASTER!" Raf yelled, gesturing violently for me to run faster.

It wasn't working.

There was no *faster*.

I wanted to yell that I was trying, but all of my energy was focused on said running.

The mountains were spread out to my right, and our house was off to my left, while my sneakers pounded the dirt and I sprinted through the trees.

"Wings, now!" Rafael's command echoed through the forest, and I threw my effort into the wings on my back.

I screamed as they swept me up off the ground, for the first time ever. We had tried dozens of times without success, but finally, it was working.

And holy shit, it was terrifying.

With panic pumping through me, my wings' movements went askew. I accidentally launched myself toward a tree, and another scream tore the air.

Rafael's thick, muscular body slammed into me just before I crashed. We spiraled for a moment, and then glided smoothly to the ground.

The bastard was grinning when he set me on my feet. I clung to him, my chest still heaving and panic still flooding my veins.

"You did it!" He hugged me fiercely. "That was perfect, Tater-tot."

"I almost hit a tree!" I clutched him tighter. "I'm never doing that again."

He laughed, sweeping me off my feet and hauling me toward our house. "We'll get some coffee in you, and we'll try again. You'll do better the second time."

"That was the *nineteenth* time."

"The second time in the air, then."

When I groaned, he flashed me another grin.

I couldn't stop the small smile from creeping onto my face. "Fine, I'll try again. Just one more time."

"One more is all you need." He tossed me onto our couch before disappearing into the kitchen. I shifted automatically back to my human form before I collided with the gloriously-comfortable furniture.

"You've said that the last eighteen times, Rafael," I called over my shoulder.

"And I'll say it the next eighteen, too," he called back.

My stubborn smile grew just a little more.

He came back two minutes later with a cup of coffee I knew was perfect, even without tasting it. A taste made me sigh in bliss, and proved me right.

Raf tucked me against his chest, plopping a kiss on my hair. "You looked good out there, terror aside."

I smiled reluctantly, leaning closer to him. "Thanks for making me do this. Despite all my complaining, I'm glad I'm learning."

"Of course." He stole my coffee, taking a quick drink before handing it back. The man didn't go through nearly as much chocolate as he used to, though he still had a killer sweet tooth. "We're heading to London in the morning, so we've got to get you flying tonight."

I sighed, and he grinned.

After taking another long sip of the drink, I finally handed it back to him. "Let's do this."

He dropped the coffee on the table, scooped me up off the couch, and tossed me over his shoulder. A laugh escaped me as he strode toward the door, and I couldn't help but check out the view.

Damn, his ass looked good in joggers.

His hand landed on my butt, and squeezed. "I can see your lust, Tater-tot. Reign it in before I'm given no choice but to take you against a tree."

"Is that supposed to be a threat?"

"Nah, it's a promise." He smacked my ass, then set me down on my feet. "Fly for me, Tater-tot, then we'll make love."

With a grin, I spread my wings. Those hot, blue eyes ran over me in my demon form, and I took off running again.

Life as a Villin was a hell of a lot of fun.

afterthoughts

So, this book happened.
Yep.
Wow.
It was unexpected, to say the least. Severely unexpected.
But honestly?
I've felt better writing it than I have in a long time. I smiled more. I grinned more. I laughed at more of my stupid jokes.
And I had fun.
So damn much fun.
This is why I love books—because they make me happy. And I hope they make you happy, too.
Will Miley, Brynn, Zander, and Bash have their own stories?
And will they perhaps overlap?
Yeppppp.
I'm in the business of happily-ever-afters these days, after all.
Miles's story will be up next, in *How to Fall in Like with a Monster*, and Brynn's will come third, in *How to Fall in Lust with a Devil.*

Have you figured out which of them is going to end up with which brother? I had fun playing with the possibilities ;)

Anyway, I hope you had as much fun in Scale Ridge as I did!

As always, thanks for reading!

All the love,

Lola Glass <3

stay in touch

If you want to receive Lola's newsletter for new releases (no spam!) use this link:

LINK

Or find her on:
FACEBOOK
TIKTOK
INSTAGRAM
PINTEREST
GOODREADS

all series by lola glass

Standalones:

Deceit and Devotion

Claimed by the Wolf

Forbidden Mates

Wild Hunt

Kings of Disaster

Night's Curse

Outcast Pack

Feral Pack

Mate Hunt

Series:

Burning Kingdom

Sacrificed to the Fae King

Shifter Queen

Wolfsbane

Shifter City

Supernatural Underworld

Moon of the Monsters
Rejected Mate Refuge

please review

Here it is. The awkward page at the end of the book where the author begs you to leave a review.
Believe me, I hate it more than you do.
But, this is me swallowing my pride and asking.
Whether you loved or hated this story, you made it this far, so please review! Your reviews play a MASSIVE role in determining whether others read my books, and ultimately, writing is a job for me—even if it's the best job ever—so I write what people are reading.
Regardless of whether you do or not, thank you so much for reading <3
-Lola

about the author

Lola is a book-lover with a *slight* romance obsession and a passion for love—real love. Not the flowers-and-chocolates kind of love, but the kind where two people build a relationship strong enough to last. That's the kind of relationship she loves to read about, and the kind she tries to portray in her books.

Even though they're fun stories about sassy women and huge, growly magical men ;)

Milton Keynes UK
Ingram Content Group UK Ltd.
UKHW041816110724
445508UK00001B/8